THE POISONS OF GOODLADIES ROAD

A Timberdick Mystery

Malcolm Noble

Matador
9 Priory Business Park
Kibworth Beauchamp
Leicestershire LE8 0RX, UK
Tel: (+44) 116 279 2299
Fax: (+44) 116 279 2277
Email: books@troubador.co.uk
Web: www.troubador.co.uk/matador

This is a work of fiction. All characters and events are imaginary
and any resemblance to actual characters and events is purely coincidental.

ISBN 978 1780883 489

British Library Cataloguing in Publication Data.
A catalogue record for this book is available from the British Library.

Typeset in 11pt Minion Pro by Troubador Publishing Ltd, Leicester, UK

Matador is an imprint of Troubador Publishing Ltd

Printed and bound in the UK by TJ International, Padstow, Cornwall

THE POISONS OF GOODLADIES ROAD

A Timberdick Mystery

As a young man, Malcolm Noble served in the Hampshire Police, a chapter in his life that provides some background to his crime fiction. He has written ten mystery novels set in the south of England from the 1920s through to the 1960s. Press reviews have emphasised the author's sense of place and atmosphere, his strong characterisation and first rate storytelling.

Malcolm Noble lives in Market Harborough where he and his wife run a bookshop.

To Christine

PART ONE

The Alibi of the Stub-fingered Man

ONE

Murder on Marbles Night

The girl with cropped hair and bony shoulders had been paid to lose. She lodged the curly kinger in the crook of her forefinger, weighed it against her thumbnail, then leaned forward to toss it at the crack between two stone slabs.

Twenty hardened watermen, in rigs right for a trawler's wet deck, had come up from the harbour and joined the regular gamblers on Goodladies Road. They sat on dustbins, clung to drainpipes and slouched against the wet walls of the covered alley. They clutched at their belt buckles and hitched up their trousers. They trod cigarette ends into the fractured concrete. And when the dust got to their scarred and calloused throats, they drew up and spitted.

"She's doing it again," grumbled the American whom no other man knew. "She's lifting her feet off the ground." No one listened to him. He coughed at the back of his throat and tugged at the open edges of his camel coat. Beneath, he wore braces and a striped shirt with no collar, and corduroys with patches at the knees. His boots were years old.

When the glass marble rolled within a hand's span of the 'kimmie', Fish Marjie made a chewing shape with her mouth and mumbled, "That puts you ahead, Timbers. Stop buggering about."

This was a dubious assembly. It was 1967; marbles matches were no longer the violent rucks of the '50s with beer bottles flying and dirty handkerchiefs pressed to bloody foreheads, but respectable folk were still wary of the ruffians who took part. The two families, who lived in terraced houses on each side, stayed indoors. By ten, they

3

were upstairs and children were told not to look out. Mother Perks wanted to post the household mongrel in the back yard but Mister said it would be unfair to the animal, so the woman kept watch at the bedroom window, ready to bark at any trespass. "Thank God, they've scared the old copper away," her husband muttered from under the blankets.

Fat Fish Marjie stood at the dead end of the alley. Hands on hips, feet apart, with a dirty bandage loose around one knee, and the strings from four old aprons knotted together so that they could wrap twice around her ample trunk. Fish Marjie had been a marbles number one before the war and, this evening, she was promoter, scorer and totaliser. She lodged the takings where no man would be brave enough to search, although the old 'uns had plenty of fun picturing how the purse got there and stayed there.

Once again, she told Timberdick to concentrate on the pool of amber light where beams from three torches turned the nest of target marbles into a golden treasure trove. But the younger woman took no notice. She was determined to show off her top-notch skills, no matter that she had promised to cheat. And she would give in, when the time came, with a paddy that no one would believe. She wanted them to go away thinking that she could have won, if she had wanted.

After each throw, lewd cries of encouragement, mixed with tobacco coughs and heavy handed clapping, bounced around the red brick tunnel, a cacophony that sharpened the intensity of play. Time and again, the watermen complained as their challenger's throws were judged to be foul. "Nowhere's there's a bounce!" they cried. "Who's saying a lob's out of the rules?" They stamped their feet and wiped muscled hands across their faces. A skinny terrier, with a doubled length of string for a lead, sat in the middle of it all; no amount of barging or barracking would make him move without the word from his crooked master. But the Goodladies convention was clear. A player could bowl only once against each target; after that, it was down to knuckles and flickers.

When Timberdick stepped forward for her next throw, they tried to put her off by shouting, 'No histing!' at the last moment. Still, she scored.

The younger ones stepped away and looked for trouble in the main street. They had neither the patience nor the passion for the game and had come only because of some dirty jokes about Timbers. These were proud lads. They said that their ton-up fashions, already five years out of date, were statements of an allegiance to the pure rock'n'roll they had envied in their childhoods. But few people saw it like that. Too many thought the boys from the waterfront were a bunch of troublesome left-overs.

It was a cold evening and, although it wasn't noisy, the sounds across the city had a brittle edge; tomorrow, there would be a frost before morning. The lads showed off and cat-called. They stubbed their fags on proudly polished doorsteps and windowsills, and stuck their fingers in their ears and noses and anywhere that might be thought dirty. They taunted late night drinkers on their way home but, on that dank night towards the end of March, no one wanted to bite back.

Twenty yards up, on the other side of the road, I was sheltering in the unlit porch of a pokey shop. My neck itched because I had shaved in a hurry and cold soap had dried on my shirt collar, and my toes were tacky in my police boots. I had got behind with my laundry, so hadn't been able to air my socks properly. I had arranged to share a saucepan supper with the Co-Op's night-watchman at half past eleven; I had another forty minutes to wait. I unwrapped a liquorice sweet in the pocket of my greatcoat and popped it into my mouth. I had three left but wanted to save at least two for the second half of my shift. As I played a game of testing how long I could suck before chewing, one of the children at an upstairs window shouted, "Eh, mister! You with the 'tuffies', gi' us one." They had been told there was going to be a street-fight, and their three little faces were shelved between the curtains and the windowsill.

Goodladies Road was busy but the marbles match had knocked it out of kilter. Men and women who lived on the Secondary Modern Estate had to walk home around London Road and Connaught Street instead of cutting through the alley. Three girls, whose regular pitch was at the entrance of the alley, now stood themselves at the next junction down (and grumbled because Fish Marjie's little scheme had forced them to move). They took turns to stand close to the kerb so that their stockinged legs could be caught in passing headlights.

Someone called out: "You'll catch your death, sweetheart, standing there like that."

"Yeah," yelled the leader of the rockers. "What'd your granny say?"

The Goodladies spirit showed through. Tonight, the road was host to unwelcome guests but, although most of the locals gave them a wide berth, there was no sense that the evening was going to turn sour. I stayed quietly in the doorway. These were good people and didn't need more coppering than they wanted.

There was a rumour that Goodladies' notorious square mile was up for redevelopment. The pub on the corner had burned down last year and three of the five roads were showing an alarming list at the junction. The doom merchants said that the place was ripe for being bought up. Rejuvenation. Being made young again. What nonsense. What were the barons going to do? Turn it into another Bullring? I believed none of it.

I let myself think that this place would never change. Its feeling of permanence was too seductive. Houses and roads, pubs and alleyways, double-deckers and bus stops needed to suit the people who lived here, and the folk of Goodladies Junction with their coarse talk and swollen joints were unpromising candidates for rejuvenation. Mums and dads put up with the toughs, tarts and tramps. They allowed their children to see life as it was because, on Goodladies Road, they'd be better for it.

Mr Whithers let his poodle out, punctually at eleven, but he stayed on the pavement to make sure that his pet prowled only the bottom half of the road. Soapy Berkeley, a weasel-faced old scruff whom I had known for over thirty years, was sitting over a drain, just a few yards from the alley. He wore old clothes and looked dirty. He sat with his knees up and his shoulders slouched as he passed six penny coins from one mittened hand to the other. (Like amateur umpires do when they count the balls in an over of cricket.)

Soapy's place in this world was to watch what went on. Generations ago, his type would have sat at a gallows crossroads or survived as sedentary look-outs for local shore wreckers. 'Keep an eye on things, Sope,' Marjie had said, two nights before, and Timbers had promised him all sorts of delights, later on. (It was just a tease, that's all.) Soapy didn't look up as the youths belly-ached and crowed; he went on counting his pennies.

The bravest youth was baiting old Mr Whithers, threatening to skewer his dog on a spit. On any other night, drinkers on their way home would have challenged the harbour-front louts, but tonight they kept the roadway between them. They passed by on the other side.

A new girl got the better of them when they tried to tease her as she trotted, freezing cold, across Goodladies Junction – her high heels clack-clacking on the wet tarmac, her hands in her raincoat pockets lifting her hemlines higher than they ought to be. She shouted back, "Aw, go home to your mothers," and "You're not worth the bother."

The girl was a loud and confident teenager but she was too young to be working on the road. Her shoes, dress and coat fitted like borrowed clothes and no one had shown her how to make the best of her hair. Yes, she had given the lads the rough edge of her tongue but there was rawness in her banter; she would receive a few knocks before she'd be streetwise, and that always put a young girl at risk. Then I saw that Timberdick had noticed her and I knew that the girl would be packed off home before long. Timbers didn't want fledglings on the road – not because of the rights and wrongs of it but because they always attracted trouble.

"Good old Sandy!" a willowy lad called out.

Reactions from the others said that he was the only one who knew her name.

"How come, Al? You know the girl? You've scored there, have you, boy?"

"Yeah," cried one at the back of the crowd. "And we thought you were here to show us the Timberdick. When are you going to chat her up, Al? You said you were going to pull her."

But they were mocking him. No one believed that young Al could have had his way with either girl.

Timberdick let out a squeal of excitement to draw attention back to herself, and Soapy kept his face down as he smiled. Just like our Timbers, he thought.

Slowly – quietly, because their bravado had been snubbed – the toughs took shelter again in the alley. Their ears and noses had frozen tips, making the grandpas smile. Smouldering pipes of shag warmed an old man's palms on nights like this and kept the icy air from his face. "Youth is more smart than clever," muttered a grey faced old-timer, and others muttered with him.

Then the tea-and-sandwiches lady from our model railway club came tripping up the road. She trawled one hand through her mess of long curly hair – some was in her eyes, some was tangled around her ears and lost in her collar, the rest was sticking out at the back like a fantail. She waved her other hand in the air and, for a moment, I thought she would lose her balance.

I stepped out of the shadows and called her back from the middle of the road.

"I'm only taking pictures, Ned darling," she pleaded, catching the leather camera case on her shoulder. She was three or four stones overweight and she made things worse by keeping out of fashion. She was wearing brown lace-ups, layers of heavy sweaters and a thick, old fashioned coat. "I'll only do it if they want me to."

I knew what the trouble was. The local Echo had chosen not to publish her photographs of our club's activities. Now she was determined to snap a more newsworthy subject. Trouble on marbles night would have suited her fine.

"This isn't the place for you, Miss Dombey," I insisted, stepping into the road. "Not tonight."

Then Soapy shouted, "Whoa!" Dombey's face changed and I looked over my shoulder to see a brightly coloured Rover steering widely out of a side street. The driver wasn't speeding but he found himself on the wrong side of the carriageway. Dombey ran one way, I stumbled backwards and the car went between us. Soapy was shouting something else and I was trying to listen when I trod awkwardly on a drain cover and went down heavily on my backside.

"Oh, wasn't it a pearly," chortled the willowy Ted as he came to my assistance. Dombey was already picking me up by one shoulder. "An old car like that and not a mark on her. She looked like a gem. Better than you, old Mr Ned. What d'you say?"

"I'm fine," I said, though I didn't feel it. I was trying to pull my trousers and coat back into shape. "I didn't really fall," I insisted. "More of a trip."

"You look after yourself," said the youth. "It's wrong, letting old men like you walk a copper's beat on your own at night."

They left me on the kerb. I had the feeling that everything was where it shouldn't have been. Gloves, truncheon, helmet strap, rubber torch and toffee bag. My collar studs had come adrift so that my tie was up to my ears.

I shouted at Miss Dombey, "I'm going for my supper now and I don't want to see you round here when I get back."

She gave her horsey, halting laugh and slowed to a neat and tidy walk. Like a schoolgirl who had been caught running in the corridor. That lasted as far as the bus shelter where she could wait until I was out of the way.

I had promised to be missing before twenty past and my saucepan supper would be close to ready. As I dawdled off to the Co-Op's yard, Soapy didn't look at me or nod but he lifted a mittened hand just an inch or two from his knees.

The match had lasted for fifty minutes. Each point had been fought hard, but Timbers gained an accuracy by preferring the smaller marbles – lucky green 'curlies'- rather than the 'kingers' and 'bombers' of her opponent. She had won two sets and was ahead in the fourth.

But there was a feeling that things had gone on long enough. With each shot, the audience encroached another half step from the edges, so that neither player could make a proper aim. Then something, high up, cracked and the dribble from an overflow pipe became a steady stream; it soaked one wall, then crept like a soddening tide across the flags and concrete. More people moved away. Fish Marjie saw that the game might soon be unplayable and she urged Timbers to get on with it. But Timbers kept to her steady pace. She was determined to make a drama.

The older ones shared wise looks when they saw Marjie still taking bets, because the woman couldn't honestly lose now.

"I don't care about the scores!" The stranger in the camel coat had elbowed his way to the front. "I've thirty bob says she's coming second," he squinnied. "Look at her – all legs and bum in the air – and marbles is a bloke's game, anyhow."

They all laughed at that.

"Kick the bugger out of here," Timbers blustered. Now it wasn't only the cold that made her eyes smart and her face flush. She clenched her fists and smacked her sides, and the men laughed all the more.

"Don't listen to him," Marjie cautioned, thinking, 'Oh God. Timberdick and her tantrums are going to wreck the whole caper.'

The man with the dog stepped forward – as gnarled, as bow-legged and hunched-up as any waterman in the harbour's memory. He tapped his heavy foot on the stone path (he had steel caps on his boots and iron studs on their soles) and issued a long gravelly shout that Marjie remembered from a brawl, years before. "You've had too much to say this evening, you old mare. And we've given you let, because I and Tom Travers know well there were days when you played some fear-a-some games of marbles yoursel'. But you keep quiet now!" The pup, sitting up and alert between his master's feet, was enjoying the tirade. One jerk from the old man's wrist and he'd have joined in.

For a few moments, Marjie kept quiet. Old Dan Groucher had shut her up. She was squatting on her haunches and knew that she couldn't get to her feet without making a comic spectacle and she knew that, for the plan to work, she couldn't risk trouble so near the end of the game. But soon the fair-weather spectators wandered off and even the challenger looked ready to concede. That's when the women played up. Timberdick stamped her feet and rapped her knuckles on the floor. It wasn't fair, she screamed, playing against a man when she had nothing on but a short skirt and everyone was trying to look up her backside. She went on, disputing and accusing, swearing and finger pointing, until only half a dozen men were left. Then the street-girl and the fishwife, working and cheating together, threw the match.

10

All at once, there were shouts and the stamping of boots and the dog was loose. Snapping at legs and feet, he seemed to want to shepherd the congregation to the dead end of the alley. Grim-faced Groucher had backed off, Fish Marjie noticed, and the gang of youths got between him and the dog. They kicked idly but no one meant to strike the animal. The crowd grew tighter and tighter. She lost sight of Timbers; she called out, "Hunn! You there, Honey? Stay clear!" but got no reply. Only once did she glimpse the camel coat amongst the limbs and torsos and brawling bodies. The stranger was fighting for a chance to lock old Groucher's head under his arm. Then the old man's pup tumbled through Fish Marjie's ankles and she fell to her knees. She was pushed onto all fours. She cried out in pain. Then more pushing sent her down on her face. She tried to protect her hands and face as the men ran forward. One or two nudged her hurting legs but no one trod on her. "Kick an old woman, would you? A poor old woman when she's down?" Her hand closed over the wad of money, hidden in her underwear. Everything else could be mended but she'd not let them get at her money.

When the noise of the stampede moved from the alley to the street, she lifted her head. "Timbers. You there, dear?"

"I'm here. On the pavement outside."

They heard the Perks wife calling the children back from the window.

"Honey, he's got our cash," Marjie wailed. "That thieving scoundrel. It's old Groucher who done it!"

When the shout went up, dowdy Miss Dombey was already on her feet and running. She was twenty-two and ran like the heavy, ungainly schoolgirl who surprises everyone on sports day because of the unexpected power in her big legs. She caught sight of the tealeaf at the top of Rossington Street, but he knew the back alleys better than she did. He could have got clean away if he hadn't cricked his ankle on Watts Yard's gate. That slowed him down and there was hardly fifty yards between them when they ran into Goodladies Road again. Old Groucher was clever. He grovelled and spat and crouched down in pain, but half of it was just show and when battling Dombey jumped on his back, he threw her off mightily. She went out for the count.

11

That's when Tad Lausen, our gunsmith, took up the chase. "It was like two old bears rampaging through backwoods" reported young Archie Perks. "All barking and growling." And when they were out of breath, they'd stand and posture, then they'd carry on. "Rampaging and barking and growling again."

Weeks later, Tad would say that they came to blows twenty yards inside Cardrew Street but Groucher always denied it. Maybe he bunged thirty quid into Tad's greedy fist; I don't know. The truth is, enough people saw them struggling through Smithy's scrap-yard and could say that there wasn't an ounce of fight left in either of them. When Harold Whithers, absorbing the last words of the last programme on the Home Service, rose from his chair to close his bedroom curtains, he thought they were two chums helping each other home after drinking too much.

It all counted for nothing because at ten past twelve, Billie Elizabeth 'Timberdick' Woodcock started screaming blue murder, not twenty-five yards from Goodladies Junction.

TWO

Not Here to do Murders

Bron Corbett was the first detective on the scene. He had been walking home from a card school when two young lads, out after bedtime, shouted that Timberdick was going crazy in the alley to Salter's Yard.

"Proper collapsed, she is, Ser'nt."

"Yeah, and just like my mum says. Legs all bent and thrashing like good 'uns."

He told them to dial 999 and report that DS Corbett was investigating. Five minutes later he called in the details, using the private phone in the nearby gun-shop. "Sounds like you've got your first murder, Serge," the desk officer said.

By the time I got to the body, Bron had received unwelcome instructions. "Mr Alexander Chickenborough is not to be messed with," he complained. "Not by us, at least. Scotland Yard are on their way and we're to touch nothing until they get here. We're not to look for witnesses, or talk to the women who found him, or listen to anything we're told. Good job we don't know who-dunnit because, as sure as hell, we'd not be allowed to arrest him."

"So you'll just be keeping watch?"

"Dead sure, I won't. I'm not leaving this poor sod in the mud while the Met try to find their way through the South Circular. I've called for an ambulance. I've got three parts of a story from your Timberdick and Zelda Lausen. I don't believe much of what they're saying, but there is some sort of description." He looked at me. "Timberdick is in the clear, Ned. She's sheltering in the back of the chippie now."

I nodded without looking at the body. "Good idea."

"It wasn't mine. That scruffy urchin, Soapy Berkeley, thought of it."

"Ah," still fixing my gaze away from the corpse, "well done, Sope."

"God, he was clutching at my coat tails. His voice is like worms in your ear. It gets into your brain and you want to shake it out of there. He's enough to give a man twitch. Can't you do something about him, Ned? He listens to you. He says it was you and him in the old days, whatever that means. He's always saying it. 'You should have seen Ned and me in the old days.' The man's no better than a tramp, for God's sake, but he still insists on telling us how to do our job."

"Soapy's not a tramp," I commented.

Corbett stepped over the dead man and viewed him from the other side. (I'd seen enough bodies to know all I needed to know about them. I went on looking the other way.)

"He said that Timberdick needed protection from the Met and suggested the back room of the chippie. I said it was a good idea. I had a word with the old fishwife."

I checked my watch. "You persuaded Fish Marjie to open up? It's gone one o'clock."

He shook his head. "That was Soapy's doing as well. Marjie said that she wasn't going to serve free tea to robbing policemen all night. He told her a good murder would bring brisk business and she should try some middle-of-the-night breakfasts."

"He's done well. Our chippie's usually late opening and early closing."

Salter's Yard was one of those dark corners, close to Goodladies Junction, that hadn't been planned but was now too old to mess with. When three shipping offices had grown so tall that the lights from the main road couldn't reach behind them, no one thought what to do with the twelve square yards of cobbles and broken slabs between the back walls. The place was coloured poisonous yellow. It smelled yellow. And the men and women who walked out of here - straightening their clothes, sometimes scratching, always coughing - said that Salter's Yard tasted yellow too. Dirty water, stained by

14

old iron and lead, seeped from a cracked drainpipe. When there was enough of it to drip, it sounded like time counting down. An old scrubwoman once said that these drips were the tears of wicked fairies, trapped in the yard and starved before they could make good. The walls were so high and, with no draught, the fairies couldn't get sufficient lift to fly out. The story sounded good enough to be true. Dead sparrows had been found in the corners for the same reason. Because the slabs weren't flat, everything wet got drawn to the middle and drained between the cracks and into the mud. The mud made the slabs wobble. Just one door – it had been cut in three shapes over the years because it had to fit into a frame that wouldn't keep square. And one light, broken above the door – rotted with wet, most likely, but it didn't matter because a light shone from the four quarters of a little window, half way up the narrow twisting staircase, whenever someone was in. Salter's Yard led to the door, and the door opened to the staircase, and the stairs took you up to an attic, squeezed in the roof of the old lamp shop. There was no other reason for Salter's Yard to be there.

"Let's do some supposing," Corbett said. "A stranger like Alexander Chickenborough comes to Salter's Yard for only one reason. He's been promised some company in the garret. We all know what your girls use it for."

"They're not my girls," I said quietly.

"You know them. That's what I mean, and our Mr Chickenborough had a promise to meet one of them here. So, he steps back from the pavement of Goodladies Road. He has to turn himself sideways because the gap between the houses is so narrow; no one had ever meant the place to have an alley. When he reaches the yard, he stands still, listening and making his eyes get used to the dirty light. He keeps to the edges of the slabs, avoiding the worst of the wet. He thinks he sees a woman pass the staircase window. He thinks he sees something disturb the light in the crack beneath the door. But when nothing else happens, when no one opens the door, when no one answers his third and fourth knock, he reaches for the door handle, turns it and leans forward."

"It's all a little fanciful, Sergeant."

15

"Then, whapp, someone hits him from behind. Someone, on this side of the door. You see, someone waiting for him in the dark."

I felt cold. "They've got his name right. Chickenborough."

"Was he a yank? Sounds like a yank name."

I said, "He's an agent for one of the custom cutters. They'll make a big case out of this, Bron."

"Yeah, just my luck." He looked me in the face. "Have you been working with him?"

"Not really. Yes, I've seen him on the pavements of Goodladies Road but I'd never met him and I'd not heard his name until tonight. I think he was supposed to meet an informant. His boss had asked me to keep an eye out for him, but I don't know any details." I said again, "They'll make a big case out of this."

Corbett sniffed and mumbled, "God, this place stinks. Let's get some air."

We walked, one behind the other, through the alley and into the lights of Goodladies Road. It was the middle of the night but the junction was as busy as it had been at closing time. "My dad used to hate the junction," complained Corbett. "He said it was full of drunks and whores and people shouting from the tops of buses. What's up with them all? Don't they want to go home tonight? Look, Timberdick's story stands up, as far as it goes. She was working in the garret, entertaining a bloke she'd not met before, she says. She doesn't know his name but says he's got hair that's Persil white. We'll call him 'Snowy'."

"That's rubbish," I mumbled. "She had no time for a job. I know she's quick about it but even so."

"They're half way through their business when they hear the killing in the yard. They run down the old staircase but, bet your life, Snowy high-tails it when he sees what has happened. She's keeping stuff back from me, Ned. She's covering up for someone, which is pointless."

I shrugged. "It's not the best alibi I've heard. She was playing marbles across the road all night. That ended in a fight about ten minutes before this killing. No, Timbers wasn't meeting anyone upstairs, so don't waste your time searching for Snowy."

"Zelda Lausen is the only other witness," he said. "She's the gunsmith's wife."

"I know the couple."

He nodded. "I phoned in from the back of their shop. Mrs Lausen says she got to Salter's Yard seconds after Timberdick shouted and, she says, saw the assailant. He pushed her against the wall as he ran through the alley."

"A description?"

"Not one we can believe. Fat bloke, dressed like a fisherman. Wellington boots with the tops turned down. Black duffle coat. Mackintosh hat, big enough to hide his face and most of his head."

"My God."

"Dressed like that, we should have a score of witnesses who saw him run down Goodladies Road. Have we, hell as like? Not one. No one saw this pantomime clown. He doesn't damn-well exist, Ned. She made it up."

"I suppose it could have been a disguise, Bron. I'd say a disguise chosen by someone who knew he'd be quickly recognised. A local man." He didn't ask for further help but I carried on. "I've seen that hat, coat and boots before. And I'm sure nobody would have come across it by accident. If it means anything, Bron, it means you're looking for a man who is well known on Goodladies Road and knows the road well enough to have seen the rig before." I shook my head. "But you're right, Bron. This doesn't make sense."

"Seen it before? Where?"

I sighed. "In Fish Marjie's outside toilet," I said frankly. "And I'll bet that your supposed suspect put it back where he found it. Leave it alone, Bron. The women are having you on."

"Do you want to walk over and check?" he asked.

"Better that I didn't, don't you think?" I asked, "Why was Zelda in Salter's Yard?"

"Looking for the gunsmith. He'd been walking the dog for too long. Mrs Lausen suspected that he was receiving special lessons in Timbers' little room up there. But Timberdick tells me, 'not bloody likely'. She's never... what's the word she uses?"

"Snitched."

17

"That's right. She's never snitched him."

Bron had his hands in his pockets and his shoulders hunched to keep the cold from the back of his head, and when he stepped backwards to the window of the furniture showroom where the display lights caught the side of his face, he had the image of his father. I recalled how the gruff voice used to say, 'proceedings progress' or, 'loose ends to be looped.' The young detective was proud of his dad and his career promised to out play the old man, but there was a difference between them. Bron was easily discouraged and had no patience for routine – he hadn't the plodding skills of the late DCI, and this prompted some people to think that Bron had no time for the small beer of police work – enquiries that showed little prospect of congratulations, that part of the job that gets no further than the faces of ordinary folk. Sometimes, people said, Bron Corbett was above himself.

I saw the sourness on his face as more policemen turned up, each one an obstacle to Bron working on his own initiative at a scene that should have been his first murder case. "Who asked for that?" he muttered to no one in particular when a dog van appeared. And then, sure that I was close enough to hear, "They must realise that I haven't asked for a Detective Superintendent. They do know that, don't they?"

I kept quiet.

The police photographer arrived in his old Morris van. (It was police blue but without any markings.) I stepped aside as Corbett opened the door and began to brief him.

As I walked away, a familiar voice shouted, "Oi, you lot, stop clogging the pavement. Go on, get out of it. There's nothing to see." Soapy Berkeley clapped his hands and shook his head as he shepherded the passers-by into the gutter and along the road.

Soapy had taken time to change his clothes since the marbles match. He was going through one of his waistcoat periods. I counted three beneath the stained overcoat. The bottom one was worn back to front so that it resembled a cleric's blouse. The lack of a dog collar made him look like a man with a dubious history. He hadn't cut his hair since Christmas and the grey curls were creeping down his ears.

In 1967 such slovenliness was seen as dirty rather than arty. (The days of the beatnik were over.) Unfortunately, Soapy's bumbled speech, and his habit of fiddling with this face when he spoke, tempted too many people to think he was mad. Often, and cruelly, they said so to his face.

"Get your dirty hands off me!" barked an off-duty railway clerk as Soapy ushered him away from the empty stretcher. He pulled his coat sleeve free of Soapy's grip, then jerked his elbow back in temper.

Soapy stepped back and into the path of a middle-aged woman who immediately bounced her rolled umbrella across his shoulders. "Look where you're going, you dirty sod."

He started clapping his hands again and calling out. Most people were content to keep walking until they were free of him, but two of our younger schoolteachers glared at him with irritated frowns.

I moved in to rescue him. "Come on, my old friend," I said, plucking at his elbow. "Give these folk some room. You'll get yourself battered one of these days."

"Thanks goodness, you're here, Ned. I've got Timbers safe and sound on the bottom step of Fish Marjie's stairs. She wants to help at the counter but I'm saying it's better that no one knows where she is. I'm right, aren't I? Thank Goodness you're here, Ned. That young sergeant's sharp enough – and keen! Oh, he's dead keen. But where's his 'xperience?"

"Bron Corbett's a fine detective, Soapy. His father was a DCI round here. If people will only give Bron a chance, he could be just as good."

"DCI? DCI Corbett?" Soapy scratched his untidy head of hair. "Never knew him. Was he a meanie?"

I smiled at that. "Do you know, Soapy, I think he probably was."

"Did you babysit for the lad, back then?"

"What makes you say that?" I asked.

"Because you've always been the sort of bloke who would. No, no. I've got it wrong. No, what I mean is, if you had babysitted, you're the sort of bloke who would come back, twenty years later, and tell an old nuisance like me to give the new detective a chance." He looked along the pavement. "He's not doing well with the doctor."

I nodded, but kept quiet.

"This job needs you and me, Ned, just like the…"

"No Soapy. There never was any 'us' in the old days."

"Was too. Wasn't I your first nicking?" But Soapy didn't wait for an answer. He was eager to test some up-to-date gossip. "Hell, Neddie. Knocking off the Chief Constable's wife. I saw you. I mean, I saw you in the back of that car, just half an hour ago. I mean, bloody hell, that's some way to score. Just think about it." Now he put on a silly voice. "What were you doing, Constable, when the man from the taxes was done in? I was screwing the Chief Constable's lady, m'lord. I mean, merry hell."

"I always wanted to captain a Lanc," I said, looking down at my boots.

"Do what?"

"You said 'what were you doing on the night when the man was done in?' and it sounded like 'what were you doing when war was declared?' so I said I always wanted to be a bomber pilot. Kids think it all the time, but I was 30 in the war and got roped into doing other things so I've had to keep it to myself. But that's what I always dreamed of."

"You're going nuts, Ned. God, don't tell me that's what you were pretending when you were screwing her. You weren't making all the noises, were you?"

"Don't bellow, Soapy, and no, I wasn't screwing the Chief's wife. She wanted to meet me because she had something important to say, but we never got that far because we had an argument and she threw me out onto the pavement."

His eyes glazed as he absorbed the story. "I won't tell anyone," he said.

"Better you didn't," I agreed[1]

But my old friend was worried about me. "You're not really daydreaming about flying over Berlin, are you? God, is this the

---

[1] So much for Soapy's promise. Three years later, when Lady Brenda and I were walking away from Timberdick's funeral, she mentioned my daydream of commanding a Lancaster. The story could only have come from Soapy. She wouldn't say how it reached her ears, but the comment went some way to stalling a parliamentary scandal. (Lady Brenda made nothing of my fantasy.)

state she's got you in? God, don't tell me you're still fretting over her."

"Soapy, I hardly ever see the Chief's wife. Anyway, me and her was years ago."

"I'm not talking about Lady Do-dah. I mean Timberdick. Ned, you've not been the same since you two broke up." He looked across the road at the two women working in the chip shop. "I've asked Fish Marjie to put Luxembourg on but she won't. Can you believe it? Murder and mayhem on Goodladies Road and our chippie won't put the wireless on."

"Shut up, Soapy."

"Who was he? The dead bloke wasn't from round here. I've done some asking around and no one knows him. Little Miss Dawson saw him at the bottom where the buses turn, about half past seven, but that's all. Could be, Ned, that he was looking for someone. Did he have a grass?"

"Soapy, I'm not here to solve murders. That's work for the detectives, not me."

"Not here to do murders? Pah!" His face changed to a sorry look. "People talk to you around here, Ned. And when they tell you things, they want you to do something with it. They don't want to go into a police station or talk to the 'tecs. They don't want to be blamed for speaking up. Don't tell me you haven't got the stomach for it, because I know you had, once upon a time."

"You're going on too much, Soapy."

He sauntered off and I turned to see Dr Potts emphasising headquarters' instructions that the body wasn't to be moved.

"I know what headquarters have told you, Doctor," the Detective Sergeant was arguing. "But I'll take full responsibility. I may be out of line here, but I'm determined. I'm not going to let this poor sod lie in the mud for a moment longer than he has to."

Doctor Potts decided that Corbett's conduct was a matter for others. He withdrew and, turning on his heels, stretched out a hand towards me. "My dear Machray, how good to see you here. Just what the locals need, a familiar bobby on the beat at this dreadful time." He was red-faced and shouting; the doctor had been drinking that

21

evening. "The policeman, the physician and the padre. A powerful threesome, I've always thought. Oh, where is Reverend Black?"

"I believe, with Mr and Mrs Lausen," I said. "Mrs Lausen's likely to be very upset,"

"Yes, well." The doctor was stepping backwards, looking for his car. "Yes, well, in good hands, I'm sure." Then he put his hands in his pockets and inhaled deeply. "This was a horrible murder, Machray. At least four savage blows to the head, when the first or second had been quite sufficient to kill him."

"You can't be sure how many times he was hit?" I asked.

"Impossible to tell at this stage. That's the horrible part of it. You see, the post mortem will tell us for sure, but I'll wager that the poor blighter was stamped on."

"My God."

"Anything from forty minutes to an hour, I'd say. Earlier rather than later. Let's say, a quarter to twelve to a quarter past. Did you know him?"

"I'd never met him," I replied honestly. I asked if it was really possible to identify a man as left handed by the uneven way he shaved his sideboards.

After a few moments thought, he decided that it wasn't a medical question. "This one had been in the wars, though," he said. "He'd lopped off the top of one finger."

Corbett was standing on the kerb, five yards away. He checked his watch again. I copied him. "The Met could be another couple of hours, Ned," he called. "There's no need for you to stay."

It had past everyone's bedtime but the diehards wouldn't go home. Maybe they thought they'd get the full story if they hung around. Some people had opened up their houses so that friends could smoke on the doorsteps. Others had walked away from the police vans and were sitting on kerbstones. But when I heard a lean-faced docker say, "Money talks. We won't be told a thing until it's all decided," I realised that the chatter had moved on from the murder in their midst; now people were repeating the rumour of redevelopment. I had already spent the greater part of the week asking questions in the council offices and reassuring locals that there were no proposals. But people couldn't get the burnt out pub and the sloping roads out of their minds. Gossips on the pavements and in shop doorways were sure that the bulldozers were coming. "They're going t'build Internationals and Fine Fares," they warned.

I was moving in on one of these conversations when, without warning, Soapy was at my side again.

"You think I've been wasting my time?" he accused. "You know me better than that, Ned. Me wasting time's not the way we catch murderers, Ned. Haven't we worked together before on cases like this? Do you think I don't know what to do? I've been talking, Ned, talking to people and looking and hearing things."

"Sope, just take me through it, yeah?"

"Here's how it was. Here's Soapy's bit in it all. Fish Marjie was running a rigged book tonight and my job was to take care of the haul when the ruck started. We knew there'd be a ruck of course, so I said to Fish, we'll make it a ruck of our choosing. Bang on half-eleven, I'd kick it off but get in quick so that I could grab the money out of her undies. That was the plan."

"Yeah?"

"Yeah. I'd get in close, put my hand up her front, grab it and run. She'd fixed it for the fence panels to be loose, each side of Number 32 so that, in half a mo', I could be away and through two gardens. 'Cept those Teddy Boys got to me. I never got nowhere near the money."

"I see."

"But there's your first piece of evidence, Ned. The ruck started at half past eleven. I know, because I started it. Then, Fish Marjie shouted that Groucher's got the money and Miss Never-been-Kissed was already up and running."

"Never-been-Kissed?"

"Your tea-and-butties woman. Your Miss Dumpy-Dombey."

"Gwendolyn Dombey went after the thief?"

"Right rugged chase it was, but it ended in Cardrew Street when Groucher knocks her out cold"

"When was that?"

23

"Fish Marjie was looking after her at ten to twelve. I've got three people who are sure of that time. Mrs Ellis from the back of Stalwarts, the couple in Number 32, young Archibald Perks and the Sharp girls."

"That's six."

"So, it's six, not three. So, we're doubly sure. Anyway I said at least three, didn't I? You here to listen, or to split hairs with Soapy? Shall I go on?"

"Please."

"If you like, we can go through all that I've said again, just to make sure Soapy's got his numbers right."

"I'm sorry, Sope. Carry on."

"Our Dombey can't have been out for more than a couple of minutes, so let's say Groucher got away from her at 11.48 or 49. Not quarter to. Not as early as that."

I stroked my chin. "It still gives him time to get across to Salter's Yard. The doctor puts the murder at between a quarter to midnight and a quarter past."

Soapy nodded. "But Timbers found the body at ten past."

I was nodding too. "It still fits."

"Not really." He explained, "Young Archie saw both Groucher and Lausen going into the scrap-yard at five minutes to midnight. Like two rampaging bears, he says."

"Does anyone else agree with ten to twelve?"

"Ah, no. But it makes sense because old Harry Whithers saw them coming out. Now, he'll say it was just as the BBC was closing down for the night. He had the Home Service on and, just as it was ending, he got up to close his curtains and saw them coming out."

I considered the point. "Allow between three and five minutes for the midnight news and weather, and the Queen, of course. Sometime between midnight and five past."

Soapy nodded. "Remember, Harry was closing the curtains as the programme was ending, not after it had ended. At ten past twelve, the whole world heard that Timbers had found the body. The two men were seen going into the scrap-yard at ten to twelve and they came out at five minutes past. That's not enough time to get to

Salter's Yard – either before or after Harry saw them – and do Chickenborough in. Neither of them did it, Ned. There's just not the time."

"But Groucher or Lausen? Why would they want to murder Chickenborough?"

"It's a customs job, you said. Well, they are two smugglers, if ever I saw 'em. And what about Zelda's description? Don't that put Groucher in the frame?

"I'm not sure she's telling the truth, Soapy."

"And she's only one reason not to. She's got to be protecting Tad Lausen." He shook his head. "But neither way works, Ned. Neither way's enough time."

"Alright, Soapy. Who did it?"

"Right now, my money's on Zelda. Always go for the one who finds the body, you know that's what I say. If not her, well, Timbers is in trouble."

He waited for me to say something.

"What about the young girl who shouted at the yobs? Have you seen her since?"

"Timbers got her took inside," he said.

"Before the murder or after?"

"That's a bit harsh, Ned. Blaming her for murder just because she's fourteen and a tart."

"I don't suspect her of anything, Soapy. I was only asking if you'd seen her."

He twitched his nose.

"Who told you it was a customs job?" I asked, but he didn't think the question was worth answering.

"If Timbers is in trouble," he went on, "you and me's got to get her out of it."

Across the road was the bright light of the chippie. Fish Marjie was frying and serving at the counter, while Timberdick wrapped the orders on a back shelf. Timberdick saw me look, put her head down and doubled her speed.

I put a hand on the old scruff's shoulder. "I can't see her tonight," I explained. "People will think that I'm covering something

25

up before Scotland Yard gets here. Tell her to be in the gun-shop at lunchtime tomorrow. Zelda and Tad will know the score. Tell her, I'll speak to her then."

"Spot on, Ned. Just what I think. But she won't want it, you know. Speaking to you."

That night, old Alfie Christopher (the only surviving son in Alfred A Christopher and Sons, greengrocers) was the last person to speak to me. He caught me while I was drifting away from the scene. "We're forming a committee, Mr Machray." (He always reminded me of those boys in school who wanted to appear mature and sensible, but looked like dopes.) "We all want you to be part of it, but I said you're barred by your office of constable. What do you say? I said it to my Jenny and she said it was a waste of time asking you."

"Nobody's going to redevelop Goodladies Junction," I said. "Don't worry, things always sort themselves out in the end."

"Do you really think so?" he asked hopefully. He stepped forward, and I had a feeling he wanted to take my hand. "My Jen makes so little sense these days. Her head's so full of this Forsyte nonsense. Have you seen it?"

"It's BBC 2, Alf."

He understood my prejudice but said that the costumes were good. "For the women really," he said and nodded.

We went another few steps before he said, "This one's not like the murders we know round here. This one's got a different mark to it."

I let him walk with me until he thought that he was too far from home, on a night like this, and he started to hang back.

"Good night, Mr Christopher."

I dawdled to the old cemetery and followed the narrow footpath that was my shortest way home. Soon, the line of trees covered the moonlight and the sounds of Goodladies Road grew more distant. I thought about the evening's episode but, this time, saw only the quiet faces in the background. The young man who stayed at the corner of Rossington, observing us all. The couple who didn't seem to move but always turned up in different places. The pensioner who had spoken to no one and walked with his bicycle as if it were a pet dog. Had these bystanders picked up that same sense as old Alfie

Christopher had done? Had the show-offs been less brash tonight? Had mothers and fathers kept a closer eye on their children? What about the people in the know – the policemen and doctors, vicars and reporters - had they given any clue that this was going to be a big murder case?

At half past five, I got home to my apartment in the abandoned, falling down police training school of years ago. No-one lived there, except me. I hung my police jacket on the back of the front door. I heard it fall to the floor, once I'd turned away, but I didn't bother about it. I took off my boots and walked to the kitchen and poured a glass of milk from the fridge. Undressing as I went, I stepped back to the bottom of the stairs, picked up the boots and took them through the kitchen so that they could air on the back step. I chose a Corgi paperback from the half dozen sitting on the fridge and went back, again, to the staircase. That's when I found her note, pinned to the carpet on the seventh step. Head height so that it couldn't be missed.

'Darling. Hope you don't mind. I needed somewhere to go. I got left where I'd been biffed. Everyone seemed to forget me. Every girl's got to be somewhere, don't they say, so I came here and stayed until four. Have washed your cups and put away. Love, Gwen. Your clothes in the holdall under the stairs really need to go in the washer. Hope you don't mind (me saying).'

I carried the note, in the hand that was already holding the milk and the paperback, up the stairs to my bedroom.

I read the blurb on the book's back cover, aloud, as I put on my pyjamas.

"Who said she could call me darling?" I grumbled, sitting up in bed. I made sure that the alarm was switched off and tuned my transistor to the World Service. I set the volume low so that it wouldn't wake me but, whenever I opened my eyes, the programme would give me some idea of the time.

I was bushed.

"This case is full of missing husbands," I said. "Zelda was looking for hers. He wasn't at home and he wasn't upstairs with Timberdick. So, where was he when the murder was done?"

I was about to bed down when I remembered that rain had been forecast, so I changed into the pyjamas top with green stripes and opened the window in case of lightning. (My grandmother's superstition wouldn't go away.) Then I remembered the boots on the back step, so I got out of bed and chuntered to myself as I went down to retrieve them. "Ten-to," I said, glancing at the kitchen clock. But the clock on the landing said ten-past, and the alarm by my bed showed five-to. So I had no idea. Back in bed, I realised that I had left the book on the draining-board when I'd gone for the boots. But I was too whacked to care.

"Fish Marjie had closed her chippie by the time of the murder," I mumbled. "Because she wanted to play marbles and her husband wasn't there to play shopkeeper. That's means her husband is missing as well." I laid my head on the pillow. "Too many missing husbands."

I wanted to stay awake for the six o'clock news but, just a few minutes later, it started without me.

THREE

An Old Case

Throughout February and March, I had been busy with the Adventure of the Mousey Usherette. It was a Revenue job and they wanted me for legwork only. Their skipper had showed me photographs of six suspects, then fixed it for me to work split shifts so that I could keep an eye out for them. I guessed that they were stevedores, up to no good on their way home from the dockyard. I had already been patrolling Goodladies Road for ten years so no one would think it odd if PC Machray poked his nose over yard fences or looked out from the tops of fire escapes. "Make sure you're in uniform and make plenty of noise," said the customs man. "No one will imagine that the local copper's working on a crime case." He said that the network relied on a little woman with a twitchy face and dirty coloured hair. She met the smugglers in coal-yards, or at the back of the bakery, or beneath the awning where Fred Perks (of Number 32) kept his fishing tackle. She always signalled the all-clear with a torch which she had pinched from the Rialto. That's why he code-named her the Mousey Usherette.

I saw the suspects on most days and completed a handwritten message form which I left in the orange pigeon hole at the back of the parade room. (Our Chief Super had decided that Revenue should be given a colour rather than a label.) But my observations never provoked a comment and I had no idea how the case was progressing.

They had me working five-till-nine, early and late, with days off when the skipper judged that trafficking was unlikely. On the

29

morning after Alex Chickenborough's death, I didn't get to the police station until mid-morning, and spent twenty minutes sorting out my shifts for the rest of the week.

I was trying to sneak out of the station before anyone found something for me to do, when at twenty to eleven, the duty gaoler caught me in the locker room. The DCI wanted to see me in his office, he said.

In those days, Divisional Headquarters was a tarnished brick building between a disused stocking factory and the back of the council offices. It had a main entrance that looked like a back way in, but there was no way to the other side. Even the meat wagons had to queue at the front. DHQ was five floors of unfathomable corridors, covered with green lino and interrupted by unexpected steps up and down, exposed heating pipes with T junctions that made no sense, and doors that seemed to have been borrowed from somewhere else. Albert Blake's office was hidden in one of the dead end passages. Next door was a telephone engineer's cupboard and, next to that, a store of broomsticks without heads. Blake's was a dark and dirty room. He never opened the blinds at the little window because, he said, there was nothing to see but another brick wall. And he kept grocery boxes of old case files on the floor. Once a month, the cleaner would refuse to go in the place. Blake would promise to do better and, in an attempt at reconciliation, he would leave the overflowing wastepaper basket at the end of the corridor each night. After a few days, one of the canteen ladies would have a word with Doreen and, while not admitting to a climb down, she would go back to cleaning the office.

"Where were you!" he shouted when I reached the open door. He was stacking one cardboard box on top of another, but couldn't let go because all the files would fall out. "You were supposed to be keeping an eye on him, but you – you, with your own damn rules – went off for your meal break. God, you old basic-grades make me weep. Bloody uniform carriers, that's all you are. Here, pass me that stump from the broken hat-stand."

He used the stick to peg the files in place, then stepped back. He picked up some papers from the cushion of a battered old armchair and dropped them where the box had been. "God, man. You left a vulnerable young girl to chase after the suspect. My God, Machray, my son knows her. She doesn't just make sandwiches for your toy train club; she also works in the record shop on Saturdays."

"She's a grown woman," I insisted. "Hardly a young girl. She's well into her twenties. Nearly thirty, I'd say."

"My Dennis says she's much younger than she looks." He was out of breath but managed to say, "Makes no difference," then pushed his backside against the corner of his desk. "Sit down."

I stood still. "I told her to go home. And old Groucher's not a suspect, anyway. He was half a mile away when the murder was done. We know that he was wrestling with Gwen."

"Gwen?"

"Gwendolyn Dombey. The tea-and-sandwich lady. The Saturday girl in the record shop."

"Gwen?"

"It's just a name, Blake. It doesn't mean I know her."

"You think your friends in high places will get you out of this mess?"

I explained. "Chickenborough wanted me out of the way before he started any fuss. That was his plan. And, to put you straight, I wasn't 'keeping an eye on him'. 'Keep an eye out for him.' That was the advice. In the course of my regular patrol."

"You won't walk away from this, Machray. An undercover officer was murdered while you took time off for your supper. You didn't even phone in. You didn't book yourself 'at refs'."

I grumbled and sank into the sagging armchair. I knew these things without him telling me.

"The Revenue Men wanted to do their own investigation," said the detective.

I snorted contemptuously.

"The Chief has compromised by bringing in a wonder boy from the Staff College. He wrote a very good paper on the value of Customs and Excise as an operational police unit."

"Do we agree with that?" I asked, wanting to say the wrong thing.

31

"You know what our Force is like these days," he said. "We agree with all very good papers." He looked me in the face. "What will they find?"

"That I've been following the usherette and her fan club for six weeks and I've seen no evidence that they're up to anything crooked. Chickenborough had volunteered to infiltrate the group, but he hadn't made any contact with them."

He nodded. "Customs must have an informant."

"It could be old Dan Groucher," I surmised. "I caught them whispering to each other last week. Groucher was rarely seen around Goodladies until last month. Now you can't stop bumping into him." I added, "There's nothing to it, Blake."

"Why is it," he asked, "whenever you use my name, I think you're being rude?"

"Because you're a grumpy Chief Inspector, Blakey, and that's how grumps hear things."

He lifted a hand. "OK. OK." He put himself behind the untidy desk. "I always doubted the usherette job. Bloody Revenue Men, they're always seeing shadows. It comes from riding dark horses along cliff tops in the middle of the night, I shouldn't wonder. That's why the Super won't let me touch this murder case. He says I have difficulty working with other disciplines. He's right, of course, so our bright young Inspector Feathers is operating as number two to the college wonder boy. I'm to keep out of the picture." He raised his eyebrows. "Meanwhile, young Corbett's in a mess."

"Ah," I nodded. "The doctor has reported him for moving the body?"

"Something like that. Have you looked at my ceiling?"

"Ceiling?"

"There. It's peeling. It's not damp and it's not drying out. It's cracking. Coming apart. See, you can follow it through to the corridor and into the chlorifier room. Go on the top floor and it's just the same, exactly the same place, only five times worse."

"You think we've hit an iceberg, Blakey?" I asked.

"That's what I think." He was still nodding and looking upwards. "I'll say exactly that when the Chief Super sees me on

Tuesday. We'll need something to talk about."

I waited for him to come back to earth.

"What do you know about Corbett's father?" he asked.

He kept this office tidy, I wanted to say, and he got on well with the cleaner. "He was a good detective. He sometimes spent days, even as a DCI, sitting in cafes and talking to people. Then he would work through the night on paper work and take refs in the back office with the beat men. His lad's not like that." I didn't tell him that the old man and his wife had separated on two occasions. That was before she ran off with a bald headed youth from the Borough Surveyor's office.

He gave a long and weary sigh. "Your tea-and-sarnies girl was in here half an hour ago, trying to convince me that Chickenborough's death was something to do with old Corbett. I told her that the case wasn't mine. I told her about Inspector Feathers and the staff college boy. I wanted her to go and see them." He shook his head. "But she's difficult not to listen to." I knew that he wanted to wipe the back of his hand across his mouth. It's what he liked to do when he knew he'd got things wrong. "Do you know Herbert Jayne?"

"He used to be our collator on nights. Then he took up a civvie job in the Force library."

"He's in Mallaig for a month. Would you believe that? Painting trawlers at the quayside. Crike, I've never heard of him being outdoors before? Well, he left a message for me to ring him. I know what he's going to say. Dig up old Corbett's investigation of his Rossington Street murder back in '48." We were quiet for a few moments. Then he seemed to make up his mind. "Look, there was talk, years ago, about Bron Corbett's father and the gunsmith's wife."

"Zelda Lausen?"

"Some people said that she had her nails into him, wouldn't let him investigate the suspect's alibi in proper detail." He shrugged. "I don't know the details of the old case. I wasn't around then. But I remember that the whole neighbourhood was after someone's blood and – you know how it is – they didn't mind who swung. I've heard that the Chief wanted old Corbett to tie things up quickly."

Blake was sweating, red faced and bulging at the neck. I always thought of him as a man with a hat, though I'd never seen a clue that he owned one.

"Why not do some work in the background, Ned? Have a word with people, up and down the road. You've got a nose for this sort of thing. Just gossip? Or something more to it?"

So, twenty minutes ago he was bowling googlies at me. Now, he wanted me to be his eyes and ears on the street. I didn't say anything.

"I'm off the case." He pressed, "Remember, it's nothing to do with me. I'm off the case and you're in bad books."

As I left his office, he called out, "That was very good about the iceberg. You're thinking about the Titanic, yeah?"

But he still hadn't finished with me. When I reached the corner of the corridor, he poked his head out of his door and shouted, "Hey! Is that true? You fell on your arse, you soft old bugger!"

It was half past eleven and I had already spent more time in the police station than I would have done on a regular shift. On the stairs, a couple of dog-handlers wanted me to listen to a comedy routine that they were rehearsing for a Force do and, at the bottom, Doreen the cleaner insisted that I should listen to the noises her vacuum was making. Then I hung around the Detail Office, complaining about last night's extra hours and this morning's wasted time. In the canteen, I was too early for lunch, but the ladies had six sausages left from breakfast and some scrambled egg which they livened up with baked beans. When I was half way through, they came to my table with two extra fried eggs, fried bread and three sauce bottles that needed scraping out. No one else was in, and I sat on my own in the corner.

I had always liked the empty parts of police stations. Railway stations without trains have the same atmosphere. They are busy places taking a breather between bouts. Living alone in a rambling house like Shooter's Grove had taught me to seek out those quiet corners where nobody sat. An empty police station is full of them. (The WI had asked me to give a talk about this in '65 but they didn't understand what I was on about; the evening wasn't mentioned in that week's local paper.)

34

"Oh, Ned!" Her clothes were all over the place. Hanging from her shoulder, hitched over her hip, twisted at the waist. Her face was wet with rain and red with cold but her eyes and her smile were as enthusiastic as ever. Nothing could spoil things for our Miss Dombey. "You didn't mind, did you? I had to go somewhere last night and sneaking into your place didn't seem a bad thing to do." As she progressed across the dining room, she pushed some chairs out of the way, knocked into others and got over one by lodging a heavy knee on the cushion and swinging the other leg round it.

"Well now, Domb!" I called as she lumbered towards my table. "What are you up to?"

"Oh, don't call me that," she pleaded. "Domb makes me sound like a drummer boy in an Enid Blyton." She sat down. "I've been trying to get your Inspector Feathers to see sense," she said, licking her lips. "Ned, yesterday's death was because of a murder that happened nineteen years ago, but your bosses don't want to know. They are convinced that Dan Groucher did it, and they don't want a tidy crime file shuffled up by tales of old cases. Ask your Timberdick. She'll know all about it."

"How do you know all this?" I asked, looking over my shoulder. I could hear the cleaner in the lavatories behind us. (She was moving her picture of the Queen from the back of one door to the back of another.)

"Because I took my film into the Echo this morning. They said no, they didn't want it. They wouldn't even develop it. You'd think, wouldn't you, that they'd be interested in the marbles match just minutes before a murder. But, no. Not from Gwenny Dombey. They kept me waiting in the foyer for forty minutes. That's when I heard two of the older reporters talking about the '48 murder. They called it the '48 murder in Rossington Street."

I knew that her ambition was likely to cause trouble but how could I dampen her enthusiasm? "You see, Chief Inspector Blake can't help you. He isn't on the case," I said pointlessly. "That's why he sent you to Mr Feathers."

"Mr Feathers says I should leave it to the old sweats at the newspaper. He says a girl like me shouldn't mess with murders."

"I say he's right."

"I'm new to the city, Ned. You know that. Oh, I know my way about and I know some good people to talk to, but I haven't the sort of contacts I'd need to investigate this. Damn me if I'm going to hand it over to someone else. Can't you get Timbers to help me?"

"She found the body," I protested. "For God's sake, don't you think she's mixed up in this enough? Investigating this murder would do her no more good than it would do you. Give it up, girl." Then: "Look, I'll have a word with Bron Corbett. His father was working in the city nineteen years ago. Perhaps he told Bron something about it. Who was the body?"

"Walter Jenkins. The family lived in Rossington Street. But you can't ask Bron Corbett," she sighed. "There're reasons."

As we carried the breakfast clutter to the serving hatch, I said, "I've been thinking, Gwen. I might join the committee against changes to Goodladies Road."

"Oh, darling! I've already promised to let them have my pig!"

FOUR

Chips with a Gunsmith

Rain stopped at lunchtime, the skies cleared and people appeared on the pavements. Traffic was clogged at Goodladies Junction, chugging and wheezing, and as I walked out of the tuck-shop, Dave the taxi man wound his window down so that I could take his copy of the Evening Echo's early edition. I stood in the middle of the pavement and checked the paper, but the numbers from last night's dog meeting hadn't made the back page.

"Darling," I grumbled quietly to myself. "She called me darling again. You can't have it, Ned. She can't keep doing it."

"You're in the way," said our coalman's wife as she pushed past. I took a step backwards and watched from the doorway of Brown's shipping office.

Soapy Berkeley stood at the crown of the junction, opened his Mac and shouted to the heavens, as if he were baring his chest for some sort of sun god. It was a silly thing to do because the sunshine, though it had dried some puddles, wasn't hot enough to be worshipped and, anyway, Soapy was still wearing three cardies and a scarf from the poverty shop. "Daft ha'p'th," grumbled little Miss Dawson, pushing a pram load of brass castors from one side of the junction to the other. She pretended she was after his ankles. Soapy skipped and yelped as the pram chased him to the kerb.

Then that wide-steering Rover turned right into a side street and a succession of drivers followed, thinking that the renegade knew a shortcut. (The rest of us knew they would get jammed at the T-

37

junction with London Road, two hundred yards further on.) There was a row of discordant horns as the cars that had stayed on Goodladies Road argued over the vacated spaces. When that stopped, we had to endure that dreadful whistling tune, coming from the TV and record shop.

I folded the Echo, tucked it under my arm and chomped on my pipe.

"You can't stand it, can you?" said tiny Miss D, bringing her pram to a stop at the pavement's edge.

"It's not my sort of music," I said.

"My latest was doing it all last night, making all the marching noises. He was very funny. It's called Kaiser Bill's Batman."

"I'm sure," I said, disinterested.

She looked up and down the road, and asked, "Are you on duty?"

"I'm not in uniform," I explained.

"I said, are you on duty?"

I shook my head and, looking about, remarked unhelpfully, "I'm not sure who's covering this beat."

"I asked if you were on duty."

I explained, "The Regulating Sergeant wanted me to cover the wireless room from midnight. Then the PC who helps him changed his mind and gave me the night off. He said we could count last night as a duty shift. I've just been in to sort it. To be honest, I think they wanted to get rid of me."

Her little thin lips spluttered impatiently. "All that's as maybe. What I want to know is can you help me cross the road?"

"Oh, I'm sorry, Miss D. Of course I can."

"My Donald says the man from the Co-Op went to school with the man who wrote it," she recounted as we walked through the lines of traffic. "He says it's a signature tune for a wireless programme. That's why it's famous." She continued to look up and down the road, tugging at my sleeve. "Go now," she muttered, and "Hold on," and "Quickie-quick," so that it was difficult to tell who was guiding whom.

"You're talking about the whistling tune." I said.

"Of course, I am." She was safe on the kerb now, patting herself down and aligning the pram wheels. "What do you think I'm talking about? White Christmas?" She nodded at a couple of housewives, chatting outside the shoe shop. "He thinks I'm talking about White Christmas."

The ladies smiled.

"Dunderhead!" she mocked as she toddled off.

Then we were treated to an innocent display of mock warfare as half a dozen schoolboys staged a street battle. Lobbing imaginary grenades, firing pretend Tommy guns, they ran past the civilian population. They ducked into doorways, hid between parked cars and crawled on their bellies like alligators. Gradually, but not without setbacks, the commandos fought their way from Cardrew Street to Rossington.

"Take your shots, Jack Wiltshire!"

Another complained to me, "He never does, Mr Ned. That Jack Wiltshire never takes his shots."

"Young people, today," laughed old Alfred A Christopher (the third) as he came out of his greengrocers and prodded the shop's awning with a broom handle so that the rainwater splashed onto the pavement. He promised a couple of the lads some pocket money if they swept it into the gutters while he stacked the local fruit on upturned crates below the shop window.

"Quarter of pears," demanded a stern Mrs Harkness. She wore black lace-up ankle boots, black mittens with holes at the tips and a black raincoat, buttoned from the top to the bottom. One of the lads muttered, "Ena Sharples in Coronation Street," but not loud enough for her to hear. Hilda Harkness knew that she was being awkward because Mr Christopher hadn't got the pears out yet, but she already had her fingers in her knitted purse and was determined to stand, waiting, until he stopped what he was doing and served her.

He put a hand in the air and shouted, "Wait, Mr Machray," as Mrs Harkness fastidiously checked her change. "I must speak with you."

"You've given me all coppers," complained his troublesome customer.

Now, Soapy Berkeley approached them. "I've got bobs and tanners," he said enthusiastically, "I always keep a pocket of small silver."

"You're plum crazy, Mr Soapy," cried one of the boys. "Proper off your head."

Like much of what Soapy said, his reply made no sense and sent the lads into laughter.

Once Soapy and Harkness were out of the way, Mr Christopher took me into his empty shop. "That posh lady you were with last night," he said, wrapping two apples in tissue. "She's been up and down this road, three times, this morning. I – well, I just thought you ought to know." He leaned forward and whispered, "Old Soapy having said, like."

I frowned, and he nodded at me. "Soapy said you used to work with her, but we're to say nothing. Is that what it's about, Ned? I'd heard that you used to work on the secret side. 'The department.' Is that what they call it, 'working for the department'? I always thought there was more to you than met the eye. Sharp copper like you, walking up and down Goodladies Road – first you're engaged to Timberdick, then you're not, and you're always pretending to get things wrong. Oh, good heavens, when you fell on your arse last night. Oh, you should have seen it from our side, over here." When he stopped laughing, he added, "I did a bit of it in the war. Intelligence work, I mean. Not like you, 'though. I never worked for the department. "

His talk had embarrassed him. He said, "Well, better that you know, I thought," then looked about his counter for something to do. The shop was still empty and no one was looking at his display outside. I sensed that he wanted to tell me more, and I wondered if Alfie Christopher might have been Chickenborough's informant. If so, he was too loose tongued, and that made him risky. He glanced at the wall clock, next to a portrait of the Queen and said, "Time for dinner, Ned. You want some fruit with cream?"

"Not today, thanks Alf," I said cheerfully. "I need to pick up Tad Lausen's order from next door."

Outside, three youngsters were forming their own Long Range Desert Group. There were whispered instructions and fingers on sealed lips.

"Did you see the Rover earlier on?" asked the greengrocer. "You'll not see a smarter one than that. It used to be owned by a producer at the BBC."

"How do you know that?" I asked.

"Soapy told me."

I let some exasperation show. "How the hell did he find out?"

"Oh, he's a good detective, our Soapy. He saw the car parked in Rossington Street and showed an interest. You know, kicking at the tyres, tugging at the boot lid. The driver couldn't ignore him and as soon as Soapy got him talking, he got hold of the BBC story."

"So who is the driver?"

"Soapy didn't ask. One bit at a time, that's what Soapy says. Don't you think he'd make a good detective? I can understand how it used to be you and him in the old days."

I had no time to comment but, before I could get away, Christopher grabbed my sleeve. "There is something more," he said. "Something else. I did want to see you about the Chief Constable's wife being up and down the road, but there is something more. It's a committee. Several of us are thinking of forming one, about all this redevelopment, and we all want you to be chairman. Now, I said you'd be debarred on account of your office of constable..."

"You asked me last night, Alf."

"But the others wanted me to ask you." He was nodding as he added, "All the same, that is."

"Alf, last night."

"Yes, and I didn't get an answer, did I? But what you said about BBC 2 was right. It's too much telly. They're forcing it on us, things we don't want. Do you know, they've shown that Donald Campbell crash again. I mean, do we want to see a man dying, over and over. I said to my Jenny, it's wrong showing that boat going up in the air, over and over. And it's just as you say; it's because we've got three channels. Who needs three channels?"

I knew how he felt. The sounds of Donald Campbell's last radio message from the Bluebird, three months before, still brought back too many memories of my own brushes with death. I needed to change the subject. "Who started this committee nonsense, Alf?"

"The committee? I did, I suppose, with Groucher from the waterfront. He says we should get a pig and dress it up as the Chairman of the Council and walk with it to the Guildhall."

"Good Lord."

"Jenny's very worried about it, of course, because that Zelda Lausen's been putting things in her ahead."

"About the pig?" I asked.

"No, no. She's fretting about the redevelopment, not the pig. I'm not sure the pig will actually come off. Ah, Mr Ned, it's a bad business, this murder." He shook his head. "You can't blame the marbles match. Fish Marjie says that people got too excited but I say no. The marbles men knew when to stop their bravado. It would never have got as far as murder. Ask Harold Whithers. He was turning off his wireless when he looked out his window and saw Groucher and Lausen. He says they were like two drunken pals, arms around each other's shoulders as they tried to get home."

"I've heard that," I commented.

"Mind, he says, he wouldn't have seen anything if the Home Service hadn't been delayed because of news of that oil tanker. It was ten minutes late closing down. Any other night, Harry Whithers would have already been in bed and not looking out of his window."

Five minutes later, I walked out of Fish Marjie's with some cod roe and two lots of four pennyworth. I trotted across Goodladies Road and into the gunsmiths. Lausen had said that we could eat in the shop, so we sat at either side of the mahogany counter and unwrapped the layers of newspaper. (Fish Marjie always thought that extra layers of yesterday's Daily Mirror meant that she was giving more value for money.) Lausen and I studied the revealed offerings and argued over which had been dowsed with extra vinegar. Then we shifted the dinners around until the special order was under his nose and not mine. We tucked in, licking the salt from our fingertips after every third or fourth mouthful.

Neither Tad nor Zelda were the marrying kind. The old women of the neighbourhood said that some salacious secret was at the root of the union, but no one had come up with a story that fitted the bill. The couple stayed together because neither would trust the other if they parted, people said. But I didn't believe this antagonism between them. What I saw was an energy that egged each other on rather than got in the way. Sometimes Tad wanted to be in charge and he would come up with a malicious scheme for making money, but Zelda was the clever one. A chap ought to be careful if she ever had it in for him. Were they a wicked pair? You bet. But they were always going to be small time. Tad wanted everything but he blundered about too much; he was never going to get it. Zelda had a poisonous heart but lacked her husband's devious ambition. That's why she was good at painting pictures, I think. She infected them with her overflow of spite.

When they first opened their shop, they were already known to the police. My superiors always asked about them. 'Goodladies is a queer place for a gun shop,' my Superintendent had said. 'Keep an eye on them, Constable.' It was generally believed that Tad Lausen dealt in stolen goods but – although I'm sure that the CID carried out four secret observations between '62 and '66 – he was never arrested, nor suspected of a specific offence. So far as I knew. So the gun shop was added to the list of tea-stops that punctuated my daily patrol of Goodladies Road. Tad always made me welcome and he even gave me information. I passed on the best of these titbits but the intelligence was always treated with suspicion. Maybe the detectives thought I had slipped under his influence.

He looked like a successful villain, that was the trouble. He was a tough guy with a past that no one could nail down. He had a knack of hinting that he knew more than he did. He liked to deny things that he wanted people to believe – and, too often, they did. It was difficult to guess how well-off he was; whether he presented his rich or poor face, policemen always thought that he had more money than he was letting on. He was never linked to any trouble but the look of him said that he should have been. So the CID decided that, if they couldn't catch him, he must be very good indeed.

The shop was dark and dusty, with the black and brown colours of a second-hand furniture store. But from every corner came the smell of oil and polish and that translucent yellow fluid which smithies use. It made me think of gone-off medicine. Several sporting prints – more than twenty – had been on the wall for years. I could remember when each had a price tag, but those tiny squares of paper had been lost long ago. The Lausens hadn't sold one. The open shelves of old books were more popular but it was the thrillers and westerns that came and went; the hunting and shooting books stayed put. I had never seen him sell a gun; he displayed few in his shop and I was yet to meet anyone who had bought one. But Tad was very proud of his engineering shop at the back of the premises and he was at his most cheerful whenever he spoke of his latest commissions. He let no one watch him work (that would have been a distraction) but he would sometimes show a work in progress and, more than once, I had marvelled over his detailed drawings. (I knew that local sportsmen had offered him good money for these illustrations, without success.) Lausen insisted that he was a traditional gunsmith who made his money from his work, not from the meagre sales in his shop. He had a yellowish look, as if the metals and polish had got under his skin.

"Where is she?" I asked, nodding at the vacant corner where Zelda's sketching stool usually stood.

"She's drawing pictures in the graveyard. God knows why."

"Because she'll be good with ghosts and ghouls," I said.

"She said something at breakfast," he said. "I promised I'd check with you."

He had a particularly long chip, longer than any potato I'd ever seen. As fat as a boxer's finger, it was, with the dark vinegar and lard lying across it like poor man's dressing. He was avoiding it, skirting around it as he chose all the lesser chips. I guessed that he was saving it for last. I wondered if he would swap it for three of my chips.

"What did she say, Lausen?" I asked.

"She said that she wasn't sure but we know Zelda's always right, don't we? She wouldn't have said it if she wasn't sure. She'd have kept it to herself." He looked up from his lunch. Tad Lausen's teeth, coloured like walnuts, were strong and well-seated, but looked too big for his gums, so that he spoke like a man who couldn't comfortably close his mouth. "You want this big chip, don't you?" he suggested.

"Only if you don't."

He made a face that said, 'OK if you don't want to ask, go without.'

"I'll give you three of mine," I offered.

"But they haven't got enough vinegar on them. I'd miss it." He shook his head. "They wouldn't taste the same."

I put three in my mouth in one go and didn't speak again until I'd eaten them. I tried to nod that a lady was looking in the shop window, but Lausen wouldn't respond. He had found an interesting column in the chip paper. "Says here that the Torrey Canyon should never have been in our parts. She was due for Hong Kong but got rerouted at the last moment. What d'you think?"

He went on picking at the chips. His fingers were taut, as if bending them would make them burst, and the nails were tarnished and turned in at the tips. "Makes you wonder where these journalists get all their stories," he said idly and not even looking at me as he rubbed the greasy newsprint, trying to make more words appear. Then: "Zelda was talking about the murder round here in '48. Skinner was hung for it." He got up and went to the boiling kettle in the corner.

"Who-Skinner?" I queried. "Start at the beginning, Tad. I wasn't here then. I didn't get back to stay until 1954."

"Joe, that was his name." He poured two mugs of coffee and delivered them to the table. "It was a love triangle. Mr Jenkins, Mrs Jenkins and her lover. Mrs died from being poorly, Mr got killed in his bed and they hung the lover for it. He was the one called Skinner. They all lived in two houses at the dark end of Rossington Street, near the railway arches. You know how these things grow, Ned. People made much more of it after the beggars were all dead and

45

buried. I've heard it said that Mrs Jenkins and Joe would make love so loudly in his house that her husband could hear through the wall, though some of the stories have it the other way round with the husband and wife doing it while Joe had his ear pressed to next door's wallpaper."

"The poor children?" I said. "Were there children?"

That puzzled him. "What do grown-ups do with the children while they have their affairs? I don't know. Zelda and I, you see, have no children, so it's not a bother." His mind went on to other things, but came back to the question, and he said, "Poor little mites."

The lady outside had lost interest. Now, the two boys from Mr Christopher's pavement were excitedly jabbing their fingers at the window. They'd received their extra pocket money but nothing in Lausen's display came within range.

"They'll come in wanting my old cigarette cards," Lausen said quietly. "I'll sort some out if they do." He sat down. He still hadn't touched the big chip. "You see, it's not that I dislike the kids."

"Of course, Tad."

"All right, I'll tell you what you've come here to find out. You are a good man, Ned Machray, and you keep your ear to the ground, but sometimes you don't know what you're hearing. Fish Marjie was the first to see it. She saw it in his face before any of us. She said it even before Alfie Christopher had asked any questions. Before even my Zelda. Fish Marjie saw that this man Chickenborough was Skinner's lost alibi."

"But what did Alex Chickenborough have to do with a love triangle?"

"Joe Skinner claimed that he was miles away when old man Jenkins was murdered. He said he was with an American called Alec who had the top of one finger missing. But this Alec was never found. Some people say that the police didn't look very hard, that they wanted Joe Skinner hung."

"You think that Alex Chickenborough was Alec, the alibi?"

"You know he had been asking questions round here for two weeks or more."

But he had been looking for evidence to convict the Mousey Usherette's smugglers. I began to wonder if he had been killed for the wrong reason.

"So, you didn't see the body?" I asked.

He shook his head. "I was messing with an article."

My hand hung still, half way between chin and chip paper. "Article?"

"Mrs Sylvia Rivers of Baldwin Close, married to a Deputy-under-Clerk."

"Tad, no one is a Deputy-under-anything."

"You think I don't know that?" His thumb and forefinger put a chip in the side of his mouth, and he squashed it. "I couldn't care less." He munched. "Mrs Sylvia Rivers is very distracting and her little fibs don't matter. I think you should interview her. I really do. She'll tell you that I was playing with her 'on' switch for two hours around midnight. That's from eleven till one, and I have to say, my dear Machray, very invigorating it was. Do I mean boisterous? Yes, I do. I'm sure you won't call on her when her husband's around to hear her evidence. Even flat-foots can be discreet, I'm sure." He eyed me suspiciously. "I don't want you intruding. The Deputy-Under's wife and I have enjoyed a successful arrangement for three months, and mutually beneficial set-ups like this are very difficult to come by." He gave me a short and indulgent smile. While I was thinking that Tad Lausen had to be one of the most distasteful people I had met, he asked: "So he was then? Last night's body was Skinner's alibi? That's what the police think, yes?"

"I'm not involved in the investigation and I don't know anything about the murder in '48, so I can't say."

"I will give you some advice about that case, Ned, and it's good advice. Do not listen to half of what you hear. There were stories about Bron Corbett's old man, stories that he cut his enquiries short. People even say our Zelda put ideas in his head so that he went after this Skinner man instead of searching for the real killer. Rubbish. All of it, rubbish. You know how these legends start. The myths of Goodladies Junction, hey? There is a little bit of doubt," he showed the slightest space between his thumb and forefinger, "and everyone talks it up. But no one is able to say that Skinner didn't murder the old man. Even, that he didn't murder the wife as well. And what did our Zelda have to do with it? I'll tell you. Nothing. Nothing at all. So you go easy, Police Constable Edward Machray. Go easy with what you hear."

He fixed his attention on his lunch. The big one was difficult to ignore because only the scratchings and it remained on his newspaper. He left it alone and took a gulp of scalding coffee.

"Three chips and enough tobacco for a pipe," I offered.

He shook his head. "All that you've got on your plate and I get to keep my scratchings."

That wasn't fair because I had loads of chips left. I leaned back on my stool so that I could squeeze my hand into my trouser pocket. "I'll give you tuppence for it."

"That's crazy," said Lausen. "You could buy half a bag of chips for two pennies. I only want those few on your paper."

I pressed. "But these are here now, Lausen. I can't let them go."

"No, I'll not rob you."

I looked at the big chip. "All the time it's getting cold, it's losing value."

"You can take it now. Go on, pick it up, but if Zelda ever asks to paint you, you've got to say yes." His nut-yellow face was grinning all over. "What do you say?"

Zelda Lausen's portraits were grotesque. She painted people with headaches and stomach cramps. Colours that had nothing to do with nature burned on tortured faces and seeped from chubby armpits. Insects lived in double chins and grubs for fishermen grew out of bulbous noses. The forsaken souls who had their pictures painted could be sure of two things. Zelda's subjects were seen in ways that they didn't want to be seen and Zelda's subjects never wore clothes.

I smiled. Zelda wanting to paint a picture of me? I couldn't think of anything less likely to happen. "You'll put her up to it," I objected cautiously.

"Certainly won't."

The deal was as good as done but I tried for better terms. "Not for ever. She's got to ask before Easter Sunday."

"No. She's got until Christmas."

I bit my lip. "You mustn't tell her to."

He crossed his heart and held up an open hand to swear the oath.

"And you've got to swear it in blood."

"No. My word is as good as my blood."

I felt that I was in the winning lane now. We both knew the risks. Zelda's paintings were more imagination than life-like and, although the pictures were supposed to represent her subjects in their birthday suits, they were so obscure and out of proportion that no one would recognise the model. No, the risk wasn't that I would be recognised in any painting but that Zelda would ask me to actually sit. That would be embarrassing. However, my answer would be simple. If she sought to paint me from life, I would go back on my word – but the chip would have already been eaten.

I didn't say anything. I reached across the counter and, with my thumb and the tip of my first finger, I picked up the long, bendy, juicy sausage of a chip. "I haven't said anything in writing," I teased.

He closed the shop as I left and, when I looked back, I saw him putting on his engineer's smock.

I knew that any further questions would draw me into an intrigue that I wanted no part of. I wanted to tell myself that a nineteen year old murder had nothing to do with Chickenborough's death, or my Adventure of the Mousey Usherette or, heaven forbid, any business I had with the Chief Constable's wife.

Let sleeping dogs lie.

But I knew that Goodladies Road didn't work like that. The doubts, uneasy niggles and unanswered questions which had festered in local minds for more than a decade, would grow like bubbles forcing their way to the surface. If they weren't settled, they would multiply and mutate into tittle-tattle. They would tangle with other phony scandals (other wrong ends of sticks) and innocent people would get hurt.

First, I wanted to know what Lausen was up to. I knew that, just as he had passed titbits of local intelligence to me, he could have worked comfortably as Chickenborough's informant. Also, I knew that he had lied about Mrs Sylvia Rivers. He had allowed me to hear

49

the full address because, if I bothered to go there, I would find that it was wrong. Her name wouldn't be in the phone book, or Kelly's, or in the register of voters. If I passed the information to Bron Corbett, he would look a fool when Scotland Yard's investigators checked it out. So I kept it to myself. I didn't know, at that stage, how important Tad's alibi would become.

I wanted to take a slow walk home. I stood outside Fish Marjie's and recharged my pipe. The two o'clock edition was out. Harry Whithers was doing his stint as the corner news-vendor. Young Wiltshire, the lad who wouldn't take his shots, was trying to talk him into giving him something for nothing.

I smiled as I watched the little sketch. When he saw me, he came trotting up and asked, "Do you believe in God?" He looked down, sanding the sole of his left shoe on the pavement. "My mum was asking last night. She was nearly crying."

"You know what mums are," I told him. "It was probably over something silly."

"My dad said it was a fine time to ask on account of the murders and all"

Harry Whithers smiled at the lad.

"He'll end up in all sorts of trouble, my dad will," he continued. "Come on, Mr Ned. Do you believe in God? Yes or no."

"My teacher always said that good children do."

His face and shoulders relaxed and he gently nodded, in the way that chefs do when they decide the sauce is just right. I realised that he had found some wisdom in my old schoolmaster's approach which I had never twigged. He turned and sauntered away, his hands in his pockets, his shoulders swaggering just a little.

"The lad's all mixed up," Withers said as I walked off. "It was last night that did it. He was the lad who found Timberdick and the dead 'un, you see." He shouted, "Don't you worry about him, our Mr Machray. We'll see he's all right."

I hadn't settled to my dawdler's pace before Soapy Berkeley caught me up. He wringed his hands in his best Dickensian manner, and kept two steps ahead so that he could twist his neck and look up to my face. "You're safe, Mr Ned," he said. "I have asked questions from the top of Goodladies Road to its bottom. There's not a teashop or coffee bar that I've missed. Every paper-shouter, every ticket merchant. I've badgered and persisted. I've pestered and hounded."

"What are you going on about, Soapy?"

"No one saw you with the Chief Constable's wife. You're safe."

Oh, Lord. Surely, he hadn't asked the good citizens of Goodladies Road if they'd seen me in the back of a car with the Chief's wife?

"Soapy, what are you doing here?"

"I've come to give you your unwarranted earnings," he said. "Soapy's always on time with your winnings. You know that."

We went through the narrow alley and into the smutty darkness of Salter's Yard. I caught my breath as my head filled with images from the night before. The horrible shape of the dead man's broken neck. The way that his right hand was reaching out, its fingers at full stretch. That's when I realised that I hadn't seen his left hand. It had been hidden in his coat pocket. I knew about the cropped finger only because of Dr Potts' remarks.

Soapy made nothing of the place; he dug into his waistcoat and trousers, adding screwed up notes to the coins he found in his cardigans.

"There," he said. "Twelve pounds, twelve and six." (Twelve quid were serious winnings in '67.)

"Your feet are shuffling around in his mud, Sope. The dead man's mud. God that could almost be his blood you're treading on."

He lifted his feet up and down, as if the soles of his boots had suddenly become tacky. "I didn't know we'd come here to pay respects, Ned. I thought, you know. You and me. Business is business." He looked down, flexed his ankles, and trod backwards to the side wall.

"Business," he repeated, and quoted good odds for a dog on Friday's card.

"Your bookie's not from round here, is he, Soapy?"

""Not for you to worry about, Ned."

"And he doesn't know where this stake money's coming from?"

"Like I said. Nothing to worry about."

51

"And your informant?"

"I've told you before, Ned, the lavatory cleaner. She lives in her little cleaning cupboard and hears all sorts being said."

I sorted two half crowns. "Here's a dollar for Tidy's Mistress."

He slipped the money into his pocket. "Your Soapy's not lucky today. I pulled out a duffer in the Grand National sweep. I got a 100-1 horse. Eh, what good's that?"

"How much did it cost you?"

"Half a dollar, that's all. It's a game Alfie Christopher is running."

I tossed him two shillings and told him to cut his losses. It hardly dented the winnings he had just handed over.

"Hey. You're a good man, Ned," he said, passing me the screwed up ticket. "Haven't I always said that? A tip for you." He tapped the side of his nose. "You don't want to be walking up Goodladies for an hour or so. She's still about. Your Lady Brenda, I mean." He said, "You know she was in your flat at Shooter's Grove last night?"

"No, Sope. That was Gwen Dombey."

"Well, the posh bird's been bothering Zelda Lausen with all sorts of questions, I shouldn't wonder. And now, these last three quarters of an hour, she's been in the back of Fish Marjie's. She's got to be due coming out and the word is she's looking for you, Mr Ned. Mr Ned, you listen to old Soapy, you don't want nothing to do with the woman. She's only ever been bad for you and Timberdick. Best, you scuttle through the baker's back yard."

FIVE

The Artist at Work

Billy Elizabeth 'Timberdick' Woodcock was standing in long wet grass with her forearms folded to make a cushion for her forehead as she pressed it against the back wall of the gravedigger's hut. No other part of her spindly frame was touching, so her weight on the roughly cut slats of cheap timber had dug little ridges into her knobbly elbows. Bony bits had always been a problem for Timberdick. Her stick-like figure had so little padding on its corners that elbows, ankles and hips were always getting bruised or grazed. Her knees were more scratched than a seven year old Tom Boy's. The gunsmith's wife had told her to keep her feet together, making it difficult to balance, and the wet had soaked through her nylons and was chilling her ankles. "Zelda, I'm freezing." Her skirt was hitched up and her stockings rolled down and nothing was between. "I thought," she said, her voice croaky and muffled. "I thought when you said you wanted to paint my backside."

"Yes, darling?"

"I thought you meant draw pictures of it on paper. Not bloody this."

"I shall take pictures when it is all over."

Timbers wasn't sure if 'when it's all over' meant 'when it's time to go home' or 'when the paint is covering every nook and cranny'. Zelda Lausen was sitting on her sketching stool, precarious on the uneven ground, and mixing soil with her yellow paint until it looked like coarse mustard. Then she would wipe some from the pallet to her kitchen knife and lean forward to splodge it on Timbers' proffered cheek.

53

"This bottom, it has shape," said Zelda. She had returned to Goodladies Road after the war. She'd spent more than half her life abroad and, although she had lost most of her foreign accent, she spoke in a way that made people think she wasn't comfortable with English. "Good muscle coming up from a square base," she continued. "Without flab or wobble. Yes, it has shape. And a good sturdy overhang that holds the paint well."

Timbers banked the phrase for later. She pictured herself telling the other girls, 'There's not an arse on Goodladies Road with an overhang as sturdy as mine.'

"I shall have the pictures developed on very expensive paper and I shall sell them for ridiculous money. Say, ten guineas or twelve guineas. Some, I shall fix into good frames and sell them, even more."

Then Timberdick seemed to wake from her thoughts.

"Arse-hole!"

But Zelda knew that the name calling wasn't meant for her. "You're a jealous girl, Timberdick," she said. "Is that your trouble?"

"I've got no bloody trouble with him," Timbers argued truculently. "If he wants to make a buggering fool of himself, I think we should help him. Can't he see what she's up to? No, of course he bloody can't. That's always been his problem. One come-on smile from a fat woman and he's like a soft pudding on a plate."

"You mean his tea-girl from his toy trains club?" Zelda was busy on her pallet, but she went on looking at the bottom as she spoke.

"Serve the boar-head right. She'll bugger him up before it's all over and he'll come sniffing round me to sort it bloody out for him."

"My darling, our Constable Machray is entirely honourable, yet you talk horribly about him. Can't you two be friends?"

"Oh God, don't tell me 'honourable', that makes it worse. I can't be doing with goodness and honour. They get round your ankles and before you know it, ugh! It's like putting a jumper on when the sleeves are twisted and your eyes are closed. They tangle your cranks and levers, that's what goodness and honour do. Have you heard her latest plan?"

"No matter what it is, you will say it's wrong. You've got it fixed in your heart that she is a bad girl."

"She's only promised to get a pig for Groucher."

"This Groucher who beat her up last night?"

Timberdick nodded, her face to the wall. "He knocked her spark-out, for God's sake, and the next bloody morning, she's promising him a pig. She says she's nursed one since it was born. Come on, Zeld, what sort of girl nurses a sodding pig?"

"Doubtful," Zelda nodded. "Ah, I have much love for Mr Ned. I will be sad to see his hopes for this girl dashed."

"I'm bloody frozen, standing here like some dunce in the sewing class."

"It's the middle of a cold month, dear," Zelda said. "That's why you're cold."

The hidden patch of rough ground between the park-keeper's hut and the untidy hedge dipped away from the main paths through the cemetery, making a trap for the scallywags of wind that scurried around the women's legs. Now and again, the wind would pick up a fallen leaf and send it twirling high into the air. Earlier, one had stuck to the underbelly of Timbers' buttock and, when Zelda wafted it away, the leaf took some paint with it and she had to do that bit again.

"But you chose that we do it here!" laughed the older woman, unsteady on the stool. "Zelda, she would have been happy to do you in her cosy room upstairs, but you said, let me take you to the cemetery, Zelda."

"Because you said, 'paint Timbers' bum' and I pictured me lying, tummy down, in soft and greenie grass with my skirt up and my little bottie bare, with butterflies landing on it and flitting away, while you drew your pretty patterns on paper. I would be dreaming, like Alice in Wonderland, and you would be talking about something else; that's how I pictured it. Timbers, with her eyes shut, feeling a little bit fruity – I mean, bare in the air's always a bit ticklish, isn't it? I'd be thinking of ice creams on beaches in the middle of summer, and birds singing in the trees above us, and all that. Not standing against this bloody woodshed with splinters digging into my awkward bits, and sodding wet weeds trying to turn my toes mouldy while you jab sticky dollops on my arse."

"You make only a rambling sense, my Timbers."

"OK. I brought you here so that you could talk to me while men weren't around."

"What do you want me to say?"

"Why did you come to Salter's Yard last night?"

"Because I thought you were with my husband."

"I've told you. Never."

"Oh yes? And you always tell the truth to other men's wives? Look, I know Lausen is lying to me. He is seeing someone. And last night, close to midnight, I cannot find him and I see you sneaking into Salter's Yard, I thought..." Zelda shrugged. "I thought, I try."

Poor Zelda, Timbers thought. Surely, she was the only woman on Goodladies Road who didn't know where Tad was spending his nights. Everyone else was laughing about it. Carefully, Timbers persisted. "When the policeman turned up, you said that I was there before you. I was already in the yard screaming."

"You said it too."

"Because I thought you had good reasons to lie. I wanted to back you up. I thought –maybe, I don't know – I thought you were protecting Tad in some way. Tell me what really happened, Zelda."

"It's true, I went looking for Lausen. When I got to Salter's Yard, I found the body but no one else. There was no sign of the killer. You know that I made it up about the man in fisherman's clothes, barging past me. But I didn't want you to say that you saw me standing over the body when you ran into the yard. So I said that you were already there, that you'd run down from the attic and found the dead man. Why did you bring me to this cemetery, Timbers? We could talk on our own almost anywhere."

"Because this is where I first saw her, two weeks ago. I was sitting on the park bench, up there by the path, with my bottle of warm stout, and Miss Dombey-pants comes and sits down beside me."

Zelda shook her head. "This is nonsense. You and me, we always fib to each other. Since when you drink stout, Timbers?"

"It's part of Ned's secret store in an old rat hole beneath this shed. He knows that I pinch it, and he knows I do it to annoy him so he can't bring himself to say anything."

"One day, he will play a nasty trick on you."

"Anyway, what's it matter, what I drink? The point is she comes again and again. Not just the first day, but the day after and the day after that. Pretty soon, I cottoned on she comes here every lunchtime and sits quietly amongst the dead."

"And you come, every day, darling Timberdick, to make sure she is not meeting your Ned. But ah, the Dombey wants to save you. She wants to stop you drinking and give you religion."

"For three quid a time, she can try."

Zelda couldn't believe it. "She pays you!"

"Not at first. She wanted me to talk about the bloke I'd been snitching. That's what she wanted, and I said, hey do you want my time for some book you're bloody writing? Not really, she said but I said in that case she should pay what I charge the blokes for my time."

"Ah, you are too clever for yourself," said Zelda, still shaking her head. "One of these days…"

"But all the time, she wants to talk about only one snitch."

"You say, snitch?"

"Fishing a bloke off the street and making him pay."

"I see. A snitch. And this snitch she wants to hear about is Mr Chickens-borough, yes?"

"That's the name she said. So, anyway, that's all right, I thought. I'll whisper about all the things that we did together – you know, piling it bloody on. But no, she wants to hear what he said. All right, Timberdick can do that. At least the fussy cow isn't going on about health and beauty and Bible classes. But, oh no, she doesn't want to hear about our dirty bits. I could have done a minute and a half from the muckiest tale you've ever heard. I'm perfect at it. I do all the right breathing. I've worked out when to close my eyes and when not to breathe at all. Like I'm so thrilled it scares me. I nibble my lip and groan, just right. Like, God knows where I get it from. I can get the boys brimming over. You go and ask the others, Zeld. I'm famous for it. They ought to put me in a filthy picture, doing my talking bit, and they'd make millions of bloody thousands, I'm telling you. But does Miss Dreary-Dombey want to hear it? Oh no, she hasn't got time for any of that. She only wants to know what he thinks about life. Life! Well, I can't help it, can I, if he's not one of those blokes who go on about their wives and women bosses and the usual grumblings? I mean, is it Timberdick's fault? You want me to change him so that he stops worrying about the important books he's read, and politics and all. You want me to say to him, 'Hey! Presidents and Kings listen to who they want, and there's nothing you can do about it because, hey, wake up, you're just as a nothing as the rest of us.' I go on about what he's said to me — before, during and after and time after bloody time – but Dombey still keeps pushing me for more. Where did he live before he came here? Where was he twenty years ago?"

"Well, you were here twenty years ago, weren't you? 1948?"

"Yes, in '48," Timbers confirmed. "That just what she said. 1948."

"So you would have been here when Joe Skinner was hung for murder?"

"I don't remember it," Timbers pleaded. "Everyone wants me to say that I was here, but I don't remember. First, Chickenborough wants to know. Then Dombey. Now, you. No, I don't remember."

"Oh but you must. Those last dreadful days, we had all been so sure that Mr Skinner was the murderer. Then, as the execution approached and we were sitting in the pubs and cafes, or in front of our own fireplaces, we began to ask: where is this man with the chopped off fingers? Has anybody really looked for him? And in the very final hours, when already it was too late, one or two of us were saying that, yes, we might have seen him on the night that Mr Jenkins died. Bu, pah, - squitch! – Skinner was gone. It was past time and all over. You really don't remember?"

"I was worrying about other things, probably," said Timbers. "I was very young. Like I said, Zeld, it's too many years ago."

"Ah yes, and you have seen a good many nights since then. How old are you, young Timberdick?"

"How old do you think?" she replied quickly. (That's what she always said when blokes asked.)

"I say, a woman can hide her age in her face and her hair and even her hands, but she can never disguise the years in the backs of her knees. These ones I see, Timbers, presented here for me, have very thin skin which is parched."

"Oh God and bloody hell, don't go on about it, Zeld. I'm 36." She complained again, "It's bloody freezing." The next time Zelda scraped the knife nastily across her tender skin, Timbers was sure it was to discourage further moaning. Timbers wished that she had demanded more than three quid for the hour's work. "You're after killing me, Zeld. You want my bones to break so I collapse and perish in the soddened ground. Bugger it, Zeld, I know blokes who'll pay me four times what you are, just to do-dah me for ten minutes. A quick 'un and off you go, dearie. Three quid and you're taking liberties. I've been standing like this for more than an hour, I know and don't you tell me I've not. And what about cleaning up time? Do you reckon on paying me for that? How bloody not likely is that? Even then, I shall be too stiff and cold to walk. Three days, I know, before I'll be right enough to work again."

By now, the early paint had dried hard and the bottom felt as if it were covered with scabs. Or, thought Timbers, morsels of old food for flies and spiders and mice that might want to run up her legs.

Far off, at the main gates, a woman cried out and waved a loose dog-lead in the air. Then she took off her hat and waved both. She looked too stout to run but, wanting to make the most of herself, she unbuttoned her coat so that it billowed in the breeze, as she shouted, "Here, Doc! Come Doccie. Doccie come!" Seconds later, an infant sausage dog was scampering around the artist and her model. He sniffed at Timbers' ankles and he tracked up and down the shed's hardstanding. He stood, put his nose in the air and tried to work out what the smell was, and what could have produced it in the long grass of a cemetery. He snorted, and went back to Timberdick's feet.

"Keep still. Say nothing," Zelda demanded in a playful whisper. "If he does a dribble, we'll mix it with pink and see what comes of it."

"Bloody dare!" Timbers shouted. "Zelda, I mean it. I'll break your bloody nose!"

The puppy was enjoying the commotion and, tickled by the long grass and strange smells against the shed walls, it seemed that he might, indeed, contribute to the fun. His sniffing became more purposeful; he turned his back and scratched at the ground. At the last moment, sensing that Timbers was ready to lash out and wreck the surface of paint on her skin, Zelda scared Doccie-Doccie away.

"What does it look like, Zeld?" Timberdick asked when things had settled down.

"Like moonshine breaking behind a sun, with hayricks and water reeds reaching up to meet them. Today, I have to represent man's fear of total war."

Timbers pushed herself from the shed wall and twisted, trying to see.

"No, no!" shouted Zelda. "My darling you'll crack it." Then she leaned back on the stool and blessed her voice with a sigh of humility: "Quite frankly, it is a masterpiece."

"I want to see it before anyone else," said Timberdick. "You said you'd do it on proper posh paper and frame it really expensive. How many copies?"

"No more than six, that's what we'll say."

"Yeah? That means more than twenty, or even fifty, so you can give one to me."

But Zelda was insistent. "We agreed three quid. Nobody said three quid and a picture. Now, tell me about this snitch, Mr Chickens-borough. What was he like?"

"Weedy," Timbers said. "He had the look of a boy who knows he hasn't dressed properly. You know, fifty-three and still lost without his mother. But he had a temper. I could tell that from the stare in his eyes, sometimes. Miss Bossy-bloody-Dombey, she wanted to know all about that."

Zelda said, "He was coming to see you, last night, Timbers."

"I think that too."

"My darling why else would he be there?"

Timberdick nodded. "Or…"

"Or, what? What other reason can there be?"

"Can we finish now, Zeld? I'm collapsing like a bridge of paper-bloody-clips, here. Get your camera out and take the pictures."

"Yes, yes. You tell me your other idea."

"Chickenborough usually liked to do me in the Eversley's butterfly shed."

"The brother and sister Eversley, yes? The brother talks much about politics and does nothing. The sister, she is slightly mad, yes? They live where their dead mother and father lived. I have it right? So what's this 'butterflies shed'?"

"The bald-headed bloke who used to lodge with our Wonder Eversley."

"Wonder? This is the sister's name?"

"Yes and the brother is called Seraphin or Seph. Was a time, when Ned was his lap-bloody-dog."

"Ah yes," said Zelda, nodding with understanding.

"Well, the lodger walked out three months ago and left a chest full of dead butterflies in their back shed. He used to collect them. Chickie rented the shed for him and me. He liked the mess in there, he said. It was always a calamity. I mean, there was never room to lie down, or even bend over properly."

"Yes, dear. The details would be too much, please."

"He was never too steady on his feet. More than once things dropped on his head. And, bloody hell, him taking his trousers down was too bloody dangerous. He always knocked into something. Anyway, he said he liked it to feel rough and bloody ready. That's what he liked. Ouch! What are you doing, Zeld?"

"Have I asked you to spare me the full story? Now, you behave and talk nicely."

"Yes but – ouch! Bloody don't, Zelda-bloody-Lausen. Stop sticking that paint knife in my arse. Like a pointed screw-bloody-driver, that's what it is."

"So why didn't he ask you to meet him in his back yard shed last night?"

"That's the thing, isn't it? I've been thinking about it and I don't think he wanted our Wonder to hear us." Timbers shook her head. "But that would have always been the case, wouldn't it? No, he thought somebody else would be listening."

61

"But even when you went to Salter's Yard, you entertained with someone else."

"Oh God, Zeld. I don't entertain. That's what posh birds do."

"So why?"

"Look, that other bloke was never there, was he? I was waiting for someone out front - in the street, not in the yard - but we weren't supposed to meet for another ten minutes. Midnight, we said. Only when I heard you describing someone to the sergeant, I backed you up. I said I'd seen him too, dressed in the fishing gear I'd seen in Marjie's back shed. But he was never really there. We both know that, don't we? I knew, all along…"

"Yes?"

"I knew you were worried that Tad might have done Chickenborough in. If you were protecting him, I wanted to protect him too."

It was twenty minutes later, when Zelda had taken the photographs and wiped Timberdick clean, that the two women crouched behind the shed and spied on Miss Dombey.

"Zelda wants you always to trust her," said the older woman. She was kneeling behind Timbers so that she could put her arms around Timbers' little shoulders. She was close enough to whisper. Her breath tickled the short hairs behind Timbers' ears.

"Look at the way she unwraps her sandwiches," said Timberdick. "It's always the same. She looks up and around as if she suspects the birds will swoop down and pinch them."

"Is it sticky?" Zelda whispered.

"Still damp."

They watched the woman sprinkle pepper on slices of meat.

"A little tacky?" Zelda asked.

"A bit gluey on my pants," Timbers replied. "Do you think she was Chickenborough's true love?" she asked, for a giggle. "And she was jealous when someone told her that he was going in the attic with me."

"Ah, so jealous," said Zelda Lausen. "Yes, I think she is the one. Yes, here is the murderer of the murdered man."

SIX

Fish Marjie

Goodladies Road was as busy as I liked it, with clerks and shop assistants stretching their lunch hours and children pestering their mothers. Fifty yards up the street, two young men were carefully lowering a chest of drawers from an upstairs window while their gaffer shouted instructions from the pavement. Mrs Perks watched from a shop doorway; she'd give the rights and wrongs of it in the pub tonight.

A couple of girls from the junior school got under my feet as I tried to walk into the tobacconists. Each had scraps of paper, folded to make a notepad, and stubs of old pencils.

"Sorry PC Machray," said the studious-looking one. "We're doing a petition. We don't want them to knock the junction down."

The second explained, taking her hair from her eyes: "We've got to be careful because Miss Carter thinks we're doing a weed census. We're supposed to write down everything that grows on the pavement between Lausen's and here. But we can make it up later."

"No, we won't Lucy Harrington," the first child protested. "We've time to do both jobs properly."

I scribbled my signature on their paper. "Be good then," I said, avoiding two other pupils who were coming out of the shop.

"There's nothing for you in there, our Mr Mach." Fish Marjie commented cynically from the next door step; she had closed for the afternoon. She stood at her shop-front with her apron folded over her arms. "Don't waste your time going in. Are you on duty?"

"Not this afternoon, Marjie."

Harry Whithers was standing between us. "Storms at Cape Horn!" he shouted. "Chichester at risk!"

I was trying to make sense of his poster: 'Cornish Wreck. Latest'

"So you won't be wanting to come in for your afternoon nap then?" Marjie teased.

"The Government doesn't know what to do about it," Harry said, nodding at the poster. "Biggest boatful of oil, we've seen." Then he cleared his throat and shouted, "Cornwall oil disaster! Chichester at risk!"

"I've got things to do, Marjie," I said. "Things to do."

"That doesn't usually stop you. I don't know, Mr Mach, frowns and grumbles is all I seem to get from you." She said, "Chichester's nowhere near Cornwall. What's he talking about?"

"He means Francis Chichester, the sailor."

"What I want to know is, what's it mean?" said Marjie, sniffing and looking hard at the two of us. "I mean, actually mean. Torrey Canyon, what does it stand for?"

Neither Harry nor I knew the answer.

"Seems to me," she said, "that people should look on the bright side of things. Always going on about disasters does no good for anyone." But she said it so miserably that the optimism made no sense.

She turned away from Whithers. "I know what you're like, Ned Machray. If it's not your feet, it's your tight collar or damp in your shoulder. Just remember, things ain't been as good as this for years." She still sounded fed up.

I gave up trying to get into the shop for my quarter of Three Nuns Best or learning more about wrecked oil tanker.

"I've got to get home," I said, waving over my shoulder and narrowly missing a pair of young mums at the kerb.

"Look here," Marjie shouted. "The sun comes out and out come girls with all their short skirts with all their pyscho-whatsit drawers on."

"Psychedelic, Marj," I called back at her. "It's a new word. It means the colours."

Now she was shouting for everyone to hear. "Even in the papers, these days. Men! They're always taking pictures from the back and looking up girls' legs. Quite respectable girls too, like air hostesses

and good factory girls. You'd never have seen it in the Daily Herald."
She lifted her fist. "I'll give them psycho-whatsits"
Then she beckoned me with a determined look on her face that made me nervous. Fish Marjie shouting in the front street wasn't something I could endure for long, so I stuck my hands down the front of my belt and sauntered back to her

"I was trying to attract you indoors, you dozy old goat" she confided when I was close to her again. "But you're so damned awkward at being drawn into things, aren't you? Things'd be different if I was a young dolly, I don't doubt. Here, I'm not supposed to tell anyone but your posh Lady Brenda was keeping me from other things for forty minutes this lunchtime. She made me take her into my backroom, too. I could tell she was wanting to be quiet about it. It makes a woman like me ask why and what's it all about. Why would it be a secret?"

"Quiet about what, Marjie? What secret?"

"Well, that's just it. She wouldn't tell me. Well madam, I thought, if I'm getting nowhere with you, you're getting nowhere with me. I as good as threw her out, that's what I did." Still, she was puzzled. "But why is it so secret?"

"I can't say, Marjie. Do you think you shouldn't tell me?"

"Oh, I've got to tell you, Mr Mach. Otherwise, it makes no sense. Just as I've had to tell my mum and the girls who work for me. That's three now, you know. Shiel's on Tuesday. Roselle's on Saturdays and Diane's still on Friday with Saturday nights extra. It's not that they need to know but if they're going to know, I'd rather they knowed it from me. And you know what girls are, these days. They'll each have a best friend they share everything with, and they'll have to tell their boyfriends, because it'll make them sound special. And my mother, oh, she's that proud. The Chief Constable's wife being close friends with my Marjorie, she'll be thinking. I'm sure she's been on the telephone ever since I said not to."

"Lady Brenda's not anywhere around, is he?" I asked, anxiously looking over my shoulder. "It's quite important that she doesn't catch up with me for a couple of days. We've had a bit of an argument. It doesn't do, arguing with the Chief Constable's wife, does it?" I added, trying to make light of it. "I can't afford to speak with her, Marje. A little scheme I've got cooking; it wouldn't do to get too much attention from my superiors. I hope you understand."

"Do you think she could help?" she asked. "I mean, with the committee. Come now, she must know important people, being as she's the Chief Constable's wife." Then she said, more suspiciously, "What were you doing with her when the murder was done? Soapy says you were in the back of her car."

"Nothing, Marjie. Soapy exaggerates."

"I wish someone would take me in the back of their car. Back seat of the cinema would be nice."

"What have you got to tell me, Marjie? You said I needed to know."

She said, still thinking about the back seat of the Rialto, "Lady Muck wants to meet you outside the radio shop tonight at half past six."

"Have you told anyone?"

She thought, began to count on her fingers, then shook her head. "Only those people I said. Mind, Mrs Perks and Mrs Harkness will always come in if I'm short but I've not told them about your Lady Brenda's letter." She added, "Little Miss Dawson's always willing to help but she's not really up to it, is she?"

A double decker changed lanes and came in close to the kerb. A cyclist, who was holding on at the back, wobbled and jolted onto the pavement.

"Bloody fool!" shouted Marjie.

"Sorry, Constable Ned." Sean, from the ferry boats, dismounted, scooted to get going, and waved without looking behind when he rejoined the traffic on the road.

"Keep off that bloody bike!" she shouted, more ferociously than she needed. She took a step forward and set her shoulders aggressively, as if she was about to break into a run.

"Hey, take it steady," I said.

"I'm sorry. I'm a bit on edge, what with... things. Have I said my husband's not in? Yes, well. I've got to get on." She shook her apron over the pavement, folded it quickly and laid it over her arms again. She was ready to walk down the alley to her side door, but she stopped at the corner and said, "I thought I'd do some nice haddock for this evening. Well, you don't want cod all the time, do you?"

I made nothing of that.

"If anyone was to come in, that is," she said. "My husband not being here."

"Really, Marje. I don't want a nap this afternoon."

She was leaning against the brick wall, with her door key in her hand. Pink faced and fidgety, watery eyed and nibbling her lips, she stumbled through her words. "My old man goes his own way which I'm not much minding because I don't have to be wanting him myself. What I mind is his pinching from the till. Not that all the money wouldn't come his way any case, but it messes my accounting up, him taking it before it's written in and out of the business. No, I'm not wanting much because what could a girl like me want." She sniffed her fingertips. "Tacky. You smell these and you think cod or haddock, vinegar and salty. What young man would want to cuddle up with that? When my old man says he's marrying me all those years ago, I said to myself, 'he wants the fish shop, not you Marjie.' But he didn't even want that off me. They call him Chip Fat round here, though I've never known why. Why, I've never known him to spend more than ten minutes a go near the fryers. Won't you come in, Mr Mach, just for a cup of tea."

"I need to see Timberdick, Marjie. I've not spoken to her since she found the body."

"I can tell you how she is and what she said, if you come in." She sniffed and ran her fingers through her hair, pushing it back from her face. "I'm supposing a girl in a fish shop ought to keep her hair short, wanting to keep the smells away, but, you see, I've always loved my curly hair and why should I cut it off? I've always said that. I've always said: cod and curls, that's what you get with Fish Marjie."

"You were here in '48, Marjie. Do you remember a murderer called Skinner?"

"I've always said as it was wrong what we did to him. I can give you the bones of it, though there's a lot that no one knows for sure. Mr Mach, I need you to come indoors."

Fish Marjie's little sittingroom was a place of half done things. Three feet of skirting, neither painted nor sanded, was propped against a wall where the handyman had left it. The coffee table was host to a jigsaw with empty patches where a hayrick and horse's rump should have been. A little brass key was lodged in the face of the mantelpiece clock; Fish Marjie had been half way through winding it when something distracted her and she had yet to come back to it. The room was hers, rather than her husband's. The one armchair had been eased and nudged – over months, over years – to the perfect position, so that when Marjie withdrew from the front shop and flopped into it, she could get the best of the electric fire, catch the right sort of light from the small side window and see the foot of the stairs through the open door. A wad of old magazines had been squashed beneath the cushion of the chair, but that - and the scorch on the hide arm and the wobbly condition of the left-front castor – seemed badges of ownership rather than signs of neglect. This was Marjie's place.

"Here it is," she said and collected a letter from behind a fake Staffordshire figure on the windowsill.

"It's from Lady Brenda," she said as she walked out of the room. I heard her making tea as she called from the kitchen, "Like I said, she wants to see you tonight, outside Weston Harts."

Marjie feigned no innocence. She had opened the letter, read it and resealed the envelope. "She doesn't say why, but she says half past six and don't be late. And don't tell anyone."

"You shouldn't have read it, Marjie."

"What's a fall back?" she asked when she returned to the room with a tea tray "She says your fall back is the Number 7a from Hopchurch Lane. Oh! You've got nowhere to sit. You, please do, settle yourself in the chair while I fetch a stool from the kitchen." She put the tea tray on top of the jigsaw, backed out of the room and returned with a four-legged wooden stool. "I call it my vegetable stool because I sit on it when I peel potatoes and things." Then, in one breath, she said, "He's not back until the end of next week so we won't be disturbed and I've nothing to do until I switch the fryers on at four. Now, what was it? Oh, yes, the murder that Skinner did."

"Wouldn't it be better if you sat here, and I had the stool? You look…"

She raised her eyebrows.

"Precarious," I said.

"Nonsense. I like to rock about when I talk."

She put her hands on her knees and leaned forward. She drew another breath. "When the Dombey girl was sitting in that chair, I thought she was waiting for me to say something about the old hat and boots. Would you believe, no one has been round to ask about them and everyone knows that the killer was wearing them last night?"

"Miss Dombey has been here? As well as the Chief Constable's wife?"

"Well, not at the same time, obviously. Do you think I run an open house? Got enough to do with my chippie, without inviting all sorts into my living room."

"But Dombey has been here?"

"Not twenty minutes before you. I was sure she would mention the old hat and boots."

"Why would Miss Dombey ask you about it?"

"Fancies herself as a young reporter, doesn't she?"

"But you mustn't tell her anything, Marjie. Really, you'll get her into all sorts of trouble."

"It's horrible, Mr Mach, like having a dead body shut in there instead of his old boots, and no one wants to talk to me about it. But no one's said so I thought, bugger me, if no one does then I won't either, and now look, bugger me, you've made me tell you. I didn't know they'd gone missing, Mr Machray. And it's no good asking because I don't know when I last saw them. Anyway, they're back where they should be now. Now and ever since six o'clock when I checked."

"What did you tell Dombey?"

"Well…"

69

"No, never mind. Just tell me. Tell me all about the murder in '48."

"Right, in a nutshell. Skinner said he didn't do it. He said he was with a man with a crippled hand, all the time, but no one believed him. He had such a strong motive. What do you say?"

"I don't know, Marjie. I wasn't on Goodladies Road in 1948."

"Yes, that's what you said." She leaned forward again, and shook her head. "But you were in the middle of the great street-fight of '37," she said. "And didn't you find the church clerk's body in the Palfreyman, that same year. I always thought it was you who sent those women to the gallows. Am I wrong?"

I hadn't the strength to answer that question. I said, "I left the city during the war."

"But you came back after war. I know you were here."

"For a few months, yes, and I wasn't a policeman then."

"But this was '48, so surely you knew the Jenkins. They lived in Rossington."

"I was here for only a few weeks and it's difficult to be sure who I was with and what I did. Look, it was a very mixed up time of my life." Now, she had me feeling that I was rowing for a safe shore. I was saying, "I've made up my mind not to have anything to do with murders or investigations."

"But you want to know about Mr Skinner, just so no injustice is done."

"Yes, just that," I said, grateful for the life-buoy.

"You want to watch from the sidelines like a good parish constable."

"Yes," I repeated. "Just like that."

"You can remember what it was like in those difficult years after the war. Things were hand to mouth on Goodladies Road. The Hoboken Arms was still bombed out. The little shops struggled; some had next to nothing in them. Every day, you'd see the same people, sitting in their shop doorways, trying to talk customers in. That's when my father put fryers in an old army cooking van, and started our business. Round here was held together by two or three strong characters. Maggie McKinley, you knew her. And a tough old Chief Inspector who used to run police surgeries in the back of the old taxi office. He got the sack, later on. We all had little places where we could meet up. A silly one-room tea-shop in Chestnut Alley (that was Ma Shipley's sittingroom, really) and the Methodist Hall started to open in the afternoons, or was that later? Yes, that was later in the 50s. Well now, you won't know this but one of the lads from my old elementary school opened a garage on the old bombsite. 'Motor Mechanic and Springsmith' he called himself. The blokes used to meet in there and smoke and talk. That's how Joe Skinner met old man Jenkins."

She went to the great sideboard, which must surely have been designed for a substantial household, and kicked its left-hand panel. Then she put her bodyweight over the centre and one of the doors swung open. Like the trick mechanism to a secret tunnel. Fish Marjie got down on her knees and went forward into the cupboard, showing her stocking tops and plump white thighs. "In here," came the muffled voice. "Beneath the teacloths that came in Aunt Edie's hamper. Ah, yes." She crawled backwards, dragging a home-made photograph album across the carpet.

Having regained her position on the wobbly stool, she turned the leaves. "No. This isn't the one I wanted, but see him." (I was too far away to see any of the pictures which, anyway, were upside down and tipped towards Marjie's ample chest.) "No, it's gone. No, it's here. Do you see? Ginnie and her husband on Clacton beach." She put her face down to examine the picture closely. "No. Skinner's not there. But you see her? Her, with her face twisted and angry. See her? That's our Timberdick, I'm sure of it. On Clacton beach, not five years after the war. Well, it wasn't long before Joe Skinner was having an affair with Ginny Jenkins. Plenty went on between them, and Mr Jenkins knew all of it. Six weeks after Ginny died, her husband was found poisoned in his bed."

"Who found him?" I asked.

She buried her face. "No one will thank you for meddling in this. It was Jackie Wiltshire's dad. He found the children wailing on the pavement with the front door open. He went upstairs and found Wally Jenkins dead in his bed. Oh, it was a horrid day."

"Meddling, Marjie? How would I be meddling?"

"With the Wiltshires, I mean. They've done so much for that lad and they didn't have to."

"I won't be meddling," I promised.

"Joe Skinner was arrested straightaway at the railway station. He said that he'd been drinking with a man in the countryside. They'd left it so late that he'd spent the night at this bloke's home. That was the first mention of it, the alibi of the stub-fingered man. He was able to identify the farmhouse, but the owners said they knew nothing about any such man. Skinner tried to persuade people that the witness had been sleeping rough for weeks in an outhouse, but it all sounded like one story made up after another. We all thought Mr Jenkins had killed Mrs Jenkins, so the lover was bound to murder the old man. For revenge. For justice, you might say."

"And how did Mrs Jenkins die?"

"Her stones, we heard later. Well, pneumonia in the end but mainly it was her stones."

"And they hung Joe Skinner?" I asked.

"They had to, didn't they? Mind, even in them days there was those of us who thought it smelled fishy." She laughed, "Oh Gosh, what am I saying, and me a fishmonger!"

"Who? Who thought it was fishy?"

"Well, Mrs Harkness for one, but that wasn't until her husband died. She pretends to know things from the doctor."

"The doctor?"

"He's dead too," she sighed.

"But, before he died, the doctor said something was wrong with the investigation," I suggested. "Something between the old DCI and Zelda Lausen."

"Ah, you are clever, aren't you! You've heard it already. Yes, you see, Zelda could have been blackmailing old man Corbett." Then she stopped herself by raising one finger in the air. "Mind. I have to say, this is talk that came out years later, when Skinner had been hung, drawn and buried. There was a story that the Lausen woman was blackmailing Corbett because she had a naughty painted picture of him." She pushed herself forward, wanting to read any aghast expression on my face. When she found none, she leaned backwards.

"You don't find it strange? You don't want to question why a policeman would allow himself to get into such a position of mockery?"

I asked, "Why did Zelda want him to foul up the investigation? Did she know who the real killer was? Did she know, or know something about, Chickenborough?"

"What's a girl like Fish Marjie to do when her husband's away? Who's here to look at her?"

"Why don't you take me to the pictures on Thursday night?" I asked. "You said you'd like it."

"The flicks?" she said, as if she hadn't been asked in years. "Oh yes, that would be nice. We'll meet in time for the first house, shall we? Outside? It's got to be proper if you're taking me to the pictures. That means meeting outside so as you pay for me to go in."

I got to my feet and thanked her for her help.

"You're not going, are you? Why, you don't have to do that. We all know that you like your nap in the afternoons. Doesn't have to be only when you're on duty. You're welcome to Fish Marjie's bed anytime. You know that." She added, "You're safe enough. You know Fish Marjie won't bother you, and is there a more discreet place on Goodladies Road?"

'You've got to be out of here before seven o'clock,' I remember telling myself as she pushed me upstairs to a little bedroom at the front. She had a high, old fashioned bedstead and a rickety three-legged table in one corner. It was a room without a chair. Left alone, I took off my clothes and got beneath the blankets.

"You'll want to know what I was doing when Chickenborough was killed," she shouted from the bottom of the stairs, but I didn't want to bring her up to the bedroom, so I kept quiet.

I need to explain about my afternoon naps above the chip shop. For the greater part of 1966, I had been on sick leave because of the pulling pains in my legs. Unfortunately, a Super's spy had spotted me gardening at the back of Shooter's Grove and, although I insisted that I had been driven to this labour because of the Force's neglect of one of their historic buildings, it was hinted that the old training school

73

would be listed as a non-operational asset if I remained on the sick. Apart from my apartment on the third floor, I had an office because of my designation as the Director of the Police Dance Orchestra and I kept an eye on a civil defence facility in the attic. These functions would be transferred if I was unable to utilise them. It was a drawn out business. Interviews. Reviews. Written submissions and countless checks of my police pocketbook. Through all the arguments, medical evidence was inconclusive on either side and many people suspected that I was only allowed such a prolonged absence from duty because I maintained the Chief Constable's favour (which, in turn, relied on my good relations with his wife and daughter). But the threat to my quiet little living in Shooter's Grove was too persistent for me to ignore. I pleaded for light duties (and managed to get away with that for longer than I had expected). Then I went back to work.

Fish Marjie was one of the older women who thought that it was wrong to make me walk, in my poorly disposition, up and down Goodladies Road for eight hours a day. She suggested that I should call at the chippie for a nap in the middle of each shift. Now, it wasn't at all unusual for a copper to be offered a tea-stop along his beat, but Marjie said I needed complete rest, not just a hot cuppa. I want to make it clear; although she insisted that I should undress properly before getting into her bed, and although she often popped in with tea and biscuits or, curiously, a baby dish of porridge, and although she wasn't shy of walking into the bedroom, showing much more of herself than might be thought decent, Fish Marjie never climbed into bed with me.

Not then. Not before. Not since.[2]

But that afternoon, I had been dozing for no more than twenty minutes when she walked into the room and announced that she

---

[2]   Ten years after the killing of Alex Chickenborough, Fish Marjie's niece produced a book of poetry by her favourite aunt. The collection gained some local notoriety because one of the poems argued that the case of *Piggy Tucker's Poison* may have led to a miscarriage of justice. Further, some mischief makers put it about that a little verse at the back of the book was inspired by my friendship with Marjie. I want to make it quite clear that I have no connection with Hyacinths in May. It is unfortunate that a copy of this volume now rests in the treasured vaults of the Bodleian Library. Future generations are unlikely to open a book of so little consequence but that prospect has kept me awake on several winter nights. My taste in gentleman's underwear has always been conventional.

needed to change. "You'll want to know what I was doing when Mr Chickenborough was killed," she repeated as she sat on the corner of the mattress and twisted to undo the zip at the back of her dress.

I kept my head. "Before that, I asked if Zelda had known Chickenborough in the old days."

But she ignored me. "Soapy says that the marbles fight started at half past eleven and I don't know anything that would make that a lie. I didn't see the goings of Chickenborough, or Groucher or Soapy. All I know is that when I shouted 'Groucher's pinched my money!' the Dombey woman was already on her feet and running."

Fish Marjie's body grew bigger with every item of dress that she dropped to the cold floor. And every time she moved, the flesh declined to fall back into place but hung around, like bits of a bus queue bobbing off and on a kerb. Marjie was white all over.

"Timbers, she was still at the top of the alley when I got to my feet but I don't know when she left exactly and she didn't tell me where she was going. To Salter's Yard, now I've been told, to meet with a bloke who'd already given her four quid not to be late. Have you heard who that was?"

I mumbled again.

She said, "Neither have I."

I don't know if her recital of the facts was a carefully studied parody of strip-tease but she persisted with awkward cricks and crocks as she undressed. Which, I suppose, was as close as she could get to bumps and grinds.

"You don't mind me changing in here?" she interjected. She was doing plenty of taking-off but I couldn't see what she was going to put on. "As soon as I got my breath, I hurried after Dombey and Groucher. I can be lighter on my feet than you think." She looked at the bedroom ceiling and sighed, "Oh, if only I had started off a few minutes earlier, I would have got to them before he knocked the poor woman over. She was still woozy and hadn't bled too much when I got there. Not like she did as I was cradling her. God, all over my smock it was. She's a good girl, you know, your Dombey girl."

Then, thank God, Fish Marjie decided that she needed to spend a penny. While she was gone I buried myself beneath the blankets and pretended that I was asleep.

"You'll want to know what I know about Zelda Lausen and old man Corbett," she shouted through the open door of the toilet.

No. Whatever it was could wait.

I didn't answer.

I don't know if she came back but when I woke bright daylight was shining through the window and she was nowhere to be seen. I could smell her cheap talcum powder masking the odours of old fish and vinegar. But when I fancied that the warmth in the bed had been left by Marjie's large body, I told myself that it was only imagination. Then I was worried that I might have said or done something in my sleep and she might have been there to hear. I had known Fish Marjie for half my life and I knew she was the wrong person to trust.

I checked that the left-overs of my greyhound winnings were still in my wallet. Soapy's sweep ticket was screwed up in the middle of the money. I tried to pronounce the horse's name but couldn't manage it, so I tucked it behind my warrant card and put the wallet away. Then I pulled on my trousers, draped an open shirt around my shoulders (but left my shoes and socks on the floor) and went to the bathroom. I threw open the window, overlooking a flat-roof and a back yard, hoping that the cold air would freshen me up while I washed. It was a cool spring afternoon. The traffic was well behaved – no hooting or screeching, although maybe it just sounded that way because it was thirty yards and two corners from the back of Fish Marjie's house. I wondered if I was cheeky enough to shave with a clean blade from the fishmonger's packet of razors.

I smiled as I recalled Marjie's optimism about the coming summer. OK, we were losing some famous names that we had always relied upon for entertainment and laughs and some shops were closing which our mothers had told us would be there forever. But that was always the case, I supposed. Lord, five years ago we had missiles in Cuba to worry about. At least the youngsters in '67 wore bright colours and wanted to be outrageous. Funny, this modern idea of students going on strike; I mean, what did they do when they weren't on strike? I always argued that this lot had grown up with the pill and free love; that made the difference. And the mini-skirt, of course. Always, the mini-skirt.

I noticed an old cut-throat with an ebony handle, sitting on top of the little wall cabinet. When further investigation revealed a fresh packet of shaving soap, wrapped in waxed paper, I realised that Marjie's man shaved not because he wanted to stay clean (on Goodladies Road, he was called Chip-Fat because people said he smelt of it) but because he enjoyed good shaving. Then, a little excitement; I read a Goodladies address on the soap's label. It had been prepared locally, no doubt to Chip-Fat's individual specification. Here, was a good man.

I decided to treat myself to one of those neglected indulgences, a wet shave at an open window.

I commenced by washing the blade in hot water (polishing it dry, then washing it again with the tenderness of a surgeon about to do business). I washed my face in hot water, not spoilt by soap, then mixed the hot and cold taps until the water was just off-cold. Carefully, I took some toilet tissue from the roll and laid it over the left half of the water, where it would lay free of the dregs but would remain wet and ready to clean the blade at intervals. (With care and practice, there was no need to renew the tissue during the process. It was, of course, important not to buy any up-to-date soft variety.) The bespoke cake lathered at once and, wonderfully, it was creamy rather than frothy. Then, having pushed the window open to its full extent, I commenced. I had long ago concluded that the best shave takes twenty-two minutes. Anything shorter would be a hurried job; any longer, and the soap would dry on the skin before it could be rinsed off with tepid water. (I decided to ask Chip-Fat for his judgement on this question one day.) I reflected that the police surgeon had not declared on whether it was possible to tell a left-handed corpse by the variation of shaving in front of his ears, but the middle of a wet shave is no place for experiments.

Fish Marjie's account of the marbles night supported Soapy's version of the events. Although, she couldn't account for those fifteen minutes between the ruck in the alley and Dombey's tumble at the junction of Cardrew Street, I knew that enough witnesses would come forward, if she had gone directly from one spot to the other. I couldn't put my finger on it, but there was something in Soapy's version that wouldn't sit well with me.

The marbles match ended in a fight at half past eleven. Twenty minutes later, Fish Marjie had been seen by several neighbours tending to Dombey. So, probably, Groucher had knocked her out two or three minutes before that. (It was unlikely to be as early as 11.40). At five minutes to midnight, young Archie had Groucher and Tad Lausen going into the scrap yard (he described them as two rampaging bears). Soapy had guessed that Harry Whithers saw them coming out of the scrap yard at five past midnight (the normal time for the Home Service to close down) but Alfie Christopher's story that BBC programmes had been extended for ten minutes that night meant that Groucher and Tad had to account for twenty minutes (between five to twelve and a quarter past). Time enough for murder.

I was about to close the window, when I caught some voices from the yard beyond the flat roof. At first, I thought that I could hear two lovers arguing over the next stage of their affair but mention of a 'last big show at Fred's place' prompted me to pay more attention.

I was listening to the Mousey Usherette and her first lieutenant. For weeks, I had observed them without any product. I more or less believed that the Revenue Men were following a false trail and the woman and her fan club were innocent. Here was my chance to find out for sure.

I needed to get closer, but I was in the middle of a shave and had no shoes on.

Working quickly, I turned off the light, settled the open shirt more comfortably on my shoulders and pushed the bathroom window wide open. I managed to pull myself onto the sink but I had forgotten to empty it and my knees dropped into the filthy suds. By the time I had got myself back to the floor, half of one trouser leg was soaked and wanting to stick to my skin. For the second attempt, I stood inside the empty bath, then leaned forward over the basin and got my head and shoulders through the open window. I tried to flop like a beached porpoise but when I waggled my legs, I got no propulsion, so I rolled –half this way, half that way – until I dropped to the flat roof. (I tried not to think of a mare depositing a new born foal from between her legs.) Now, I was outside and in earshot of the conspirators. My shirt was torn, my wet trousers were itching and my feet were already scratched by the rough surface of the roof, but I had managed to do it all without too much noise.

I kept low and tried to hide against the brick wall. When the Guildhall clock struck four o'clock, the two people below looked up as they counted the chimes. At that moment, someone walked into the Co-Op store on the fifth floor, opposite, and the light illuminated my position on the flat roof.

I was lit up like a bomber pilot caught in the searchlights. Expecting 'archie' at any moment, I weaved to the left and dropped height. "Steady she goes," I whispered, as if to a Lancaster's crew as I lined up for the objective.

Then I heard Fish Marjie shouting in the bathroom. "You dirty bugger! Can't you empty the sink when you've finished!"

I twisted around and raised an arm, wanting to keep her quiet, but that movement pushed me beyond the edge of the roof. I felt rough, cold air rush across my bare stomach and chest. I thought that I had stopped myself falling by grabbing the top of a drainpipe. But the rotten casting gave way. My feet and elbows slammed against the wall as I tumbled down. Two feet from the ground, the tattered shirt, which had caught on the broken pipe, wrapped itself around my neck. The usherette and her mate stared at me; I was hanging with my feet loose and my face turning blue. Then, after countless seconds of astonishment, she screamed.

They ran off, leaving me choking and scrabbling for some sort of foothold.

Then Miss Dombey stepped quietly from the shadows, shaking her head and smiling. She folded her arms around my thighs and went on tip-toes to take my weight.

"This," I managed to croak, clutching the noose of shirt sleeve at my throat.

She nodded, took her arms away and said, "Don't worry" as I suffered the full weight of the strangulation again. "Good God, darling, why didn't you stay on the roof?" She seemed to pay no attention to my distress but worked steadily on the tangle of knots. "We'd have learned all their plans if only you had laid low." She sighed, "Now, I'll have to start my investigation from the beginning. I was sure that I had a scoop there. Mr Ned, this could have been my chance to prove to the Echo that I can write a jolly good story."

Then I was free. I grovelled on all fours at her feet. My hands were at my throat. It felt so swollen and warped that I was sure I would never talk again. I tried to cough into my hands but hardly managed a spit.

"Ugh!" went Dombey.

Thank God, I found no blood on my fingers.

"What's this nonsense about a pig?" I whispered. Then, because she didn't seem to understand me, I said it again.

"We're not talking about Marie Eglise now." She was standing firm, her chubby legs apart and her hands on her broad, well padded hips. Her hair looked as messy as ever.

I said, still on the floor and trying to get used to swallowing again, "What sort of woman keeps a pet pig anyway?"

"What on earth were you doing up there?" Then she paused to summon great emphasis: "Half dressed!"

I tried to shout back at her but couldn't manage it.

"I was listening," I said.

Now Fish Marjie leaned out of the bathroom window. "You're a dirty dog, Ned Machray!" She slammed it shut again.

"You tell him, Fish!" yelled someone else, far off.

Dombey waited for things to quieten down. "Well, you made a proper mess of it, if listening was what you were up to. You alerted most of the neighbourhood and you scared our smugglers away before we got the details of their scheme. All we've got is a date and something about a place called Fred's."

I ignored the telling-off. "You can't just turn up with a pig. We're in the middle of a city. There's bound to be regulations." Then I remembered some long ago training. "Movement certificates! I'm sure you're supposed to have movement certificates." I needed to bring something up from my stomach but, for all I tried, I couldn't manage it.

"Oh my God! Now you're being disgusting!"

"About your pig," I insisted.

"Old Groucher's committee needs a mascot."

I choked some more. "When did he tell you this?"

"This morning."

"He spoke to you before you went to the police station?"

"Yes." She didn't seem sure. "Yes, it was before. Look, it doesn't matter when. I've said they can have Marie Eglise as a mascot. It isn't half as bad as you making a fool of yourself when the smugglers were telling us their plans."

"Help me back up, Miss Dombey," I said when I had got back to some sort of normal breathing.

"Gwendolyn, please."

"Gwendolyn, then. Please, I need to get my shoes and socks back."

But she shook her head and told me I had no chance of that. Fish Marjie had closed the bathroom window and meant it to stay shut.

"Dombey, I can't go anywhere in this state. My shirt's torn and I've got no shoes on."

"We've no choice, Ned. Come on, we've got to get you home. All I ask is don't fall on your bottom. It's too funny for words."

Together, we quickly planned a route which avoided the main roads and junctions and promised to deliver me to Shooter's Grove without much risk of embarrassment. I was surprised by Dombey's thorough knowledge of the twitchels and rat runs around Goodladies. It took us twenty minutes, hiding in doorways, crossing when the coasts were clear and keeping low beneath back windows. There was an anxious moment when a round-shouldered gent with bow legs and a cloth cap seemed to be keeping an eye on us. He hung around a corner and did a lot of walking up and down, but all he wanted was a pee. And when we crossed London Road, two ladies called out of one window, 'There they go!' I thought we'd been spotted but they were spying on a couple of courting cats, not us.

81

She got me home before five. Then, with plasters on my feet and a mug of hot tea between both hands, I sat at the bottom of my stairs while she sorted my dirty washing into piles on the kitchen floor.

"How old are you, Gwen?" I called.

I couldn't see her but I sensed that she went on working. "What you mean is how old was I in 1948? It depends on the time of year."

"I don't know," I answered honestly.

"Most of the time, three, but sometimes two."

"I see. I didn't really think that…"

"No. I know. You were just checking because that's what policemen do." I could tell that she was standing at my kitchen window. I waited for the taps to start running, but she didn't touch them. "While you're thinking," she said, "remember that I was three quarters of a mile away when Mr Chickenborough was killed and most people say I was unconscious."

As she was speaking, I became aware of a niggling thought trying to force itself to the front of my mind. It was a doubt or a query but I couldn't get hold of it.

Dombey continued from inside my larder, "The trouble is, I've turned up on Goodladies Road at the wrong time and people are wondering if it's more than a coincidence."

Yes, something about the Goodladies development. Something Tad Lausen had said.

"What are you doing?" I asked, trying to pay attention to her.

Yes, Tad had spoken of the Deputy-under-Clerk, or was it the Deputy Surveyor's Clerk? It didn't matter. Just that week, I had been discussing the rumours about Goodladies Road with a clerk who called himself the under-something, and he came from the Borough Surveyor's Office. From that moment, I knew that Mrs Sylvia Rivers, Lausen's alibi, had a husband in the office which had broken the Corbett's marriage. I was sure of it, but I couldn't work out its significance.

"Rice pudding," she said, "if I can get the bottom of your saucepan clean. Stay there. The world's a whole lot safer when I know where you are."

I went up a couple of stairs so that my knees could unbend.

"I'm twenty-two, Ned. I didn't want to spend the rest of my life on the family farm. I needed to try other things. I came to Goodladies Road because I wanted to be a pop singer. I thought that a Saturday job in the record shop would help me but Sean from the ferries says I'll never make it as a singer." She added, "Every girl wants to be a dancer but my thighs are fat."

"I thought you wanted to be a reporter."

"Sean says they'll never give me a job on the Echo but he does want me to be a disc jockey on his pirate radio station, so I'm working Thursday and Friday evenings in the Radio and TV shop. It's all good background, don't you think?"

I remarked casually, "Please don't use that dreadful whistling record as your signature tune."

"Kaiser Bill's Batman! Oh, it's great. Everyone was buying it last Saturday!"

I got to my feet and joined her in the kitchen. "If you don't become famous you can always go back to your mum and dad on the farm."

"I do miss the farm," she said. "I miss hearing the sounds of the animals when I'm in bed at night."

"Yes. I feel the same about railways trains in the distance and hooters in the harbour."

"Ah, yes. The toy trains."

I wasn't sure what she meant. "Why did you join the model railways club?" I asked.

"I like to meet older men."

They came before six o'clock when the sun was sinking behind the distant Guildhall and St Mary's church spire was lengthening its shadow across the junction that bore her name. Juke boxes were playing to teenagers in coffee bars and waitresses in make-do tabards were wiping ketchup from Wimpy tabletops. Harry Whithers was sitting on a cemetery bench waiting for his smoky-coated poodle to run itself tired and, on Goodladies Road, Stacey Allnight and Trude were sharing the last cigarette from a crumpled packet. In the police station, a desk sergeant was listening, amused, to a report that students intended to kidnap the mayor and dress him up as a pig. He told the young constable that he needed to come up with better stories if he wanted to be considered for CID. He didn't note the intelligence on the standard message pad. He didn't mention it again.

They came in old Groucher's pick-up. A tubular frame and a patchwork of tarpaulins had been fitted to the back. This roof and sides bore letters - and bits of letters - which had once adorned a News of the World railway wagon. A fifteen year old lad was inside. He'd had nothing to do until they tried to reverse the truck towards the side path at the empty house known as the Dirty Verger's Cottage. That's when the pig played up. The pig didn't like going backwards.

"Let her fret. Let her fret," shouted Groucher as he strode around the stationary vehicle.

The lad's head appeared beneath the flap of the tarpaulin. Then his shoulders. And when his arms were out, the other men dragged him free of the pick-up.

"She's got a sow's temper," Groucher said, struggling for a solution. "No dogs," he said, when Mr Tibbs and Butterfield came up with the suggestion.

"There's a donkey down at the fun fair," said Mr Tibbs, but Groucher gave it a deaf 'un.

For a moment - no more than a couple of seconds - the pig and Dan Groucher were eye to eye on the same level. The pig had a questioning face as if the commotion was as likely to excite her curiosity as much as her nerves. When she snuffled through her snout, Dan was sure that, although he couldn't understand what she wanted to say, she wanted to say something.

"Where's her mother?" he asked.

Everyone knew that he was talking about the Dombey girl but no one knew where she was. "She were courting old Ned not two hours ago," Mr Tibbs reported. "But Lord knows where they ended up."

"Then get Fish Marjie," said Groucher. "The pig'll settle with a woman who smells of old fish."

Everyone agreed that pigs had a good sense of smell.

Alfie Christopher watched from thirty yards, smoking a pipe beneath an unlit streetlamp. He had just refused, for the second time, the formal chairmanship of the Protest Committee but he was gradually taking on more and more of that role. He had asked that the pig's reception should be as quiet as possible. Neighbours kept the children indoors and, although several looked down from upstairs windows, no one called out. Alfie knew that the tactics of unloading the pig should be left to Groucher and his crew; he didn't interfere. Youths with dustbins lids, a housewife with a brace of laundry paddles and Brown Gilbert, the second-hand man, with a lasso that would never have worked, got nowhere until a fool, with Miss Dombey's lost waistcoat tied to his crotch, enticed the pig down the planks, along the path into the old shed at the back of the dilapidated house.

The job done, the helpers wandered off. Groucher packed up, thanking the pick-up driver before disappearing into the pig's new home.

Alfie noticed the bright old Rover parked at the dead end of the street but he saw no sign of the driver, so he didn't think it was important.

PART TWO

Timberdick Takes the Case

SEVEN

My Hospital Adventure

Two hours later, on Goodladies Road, a radiogram was tuned to the Light Programme in Weston Hart's showroom. Half a dozen people had stepped back from the bus stop and were listening in the wet, slippery porch. Feet in a pair of brown brogues kept the door open but no one trod inside. The shop's clock was wrong and the manager was sure that it had already passed closing time, but he let the wireless play on, through the weather forecast and into Wilfred Pickles.

Each announcement about the Torrey Canyon seemed worse than the previous bulletin. As the gathering listened, in a dreary mood, a little voice from the middle echoed Harry Whithers' cynicism: "The government doesn't know what to do about it."

"Napalm's what they need," said an old soldier. "It's the only thing that'll sort it."

"Don't be daft. We ain't got napalm."

"Then we'll have to borrow some from the yanks. We'd only need a couple of buckets. It's strong stuff."

A housewife with rollers beneath a headscarf attached herself to the edge of the group. She had her cold hands tucked in the armpits of her overcoat. "I always wanted to go to Cornwall for my honeymoon," she said. "But my old man insisted on Guernsey."

"Yeah, and you're always saying he insists on Thursdays."

But the humour drew only a little laughter. Someone at the back chuckled. "Yeah, well, it were her honeymoon, weren't it?"

Soapy Berkeley had travelled on a bus platform from the Admiral of the Nore and, a few seconds before it stopped at Goodladies

Junction, he thanked the conductor for the free ride and skipped off. The folk broke away from Weston's and carefully re-ordered themselves in the priority that had been in play before the newscast. They filed on board; the conductor hung out the back, holding onto the chrome grab rail.

"Hold very tight please," joked one of the passengers and pressed the bell.

"Oi! You there! You can't do that!"

Then the traffic slowed so that the bus could pull away, and Soapy hurried across the busy road to the other pavement.

Already, it was a chilly evening. I had been called in to walk the six to two shift with thirty-minute points at the Basing Row and Cardrew Street telephone boxes. I kept away from the gunsmith's and Salter's Yard, but made sure that I was never very far from the chippie. I knew that Fish Marjie's women, who worked in her back kitchen, would have tea and a bun for me whenever I wanted a ten minute break. Mrs P (Perks) and Mrs H (Harkness) were on duty tonight.

As early as eight o'clock, I caught sight of Timberdick, standing on her little bit of pavement, although I was careful that she wouldn't notice I'd noticed. She was as brash, rude and as talkative as ever – irritating the other girls with her big-headed opinions and making the most of any encouragement from male passers-by. She wore pink high-heels, dark stockings and a pink plastic raincoat, which she kept closed by pushing her hands in its pockets. I guessed that she had little or nothing on underneath. Everything she did – a toss of her head, twists and turn, a flick of her heels – was as loud as the roughest shout from stallholders on Wednesday's street-market. She'd had short hair for as long as I'd known her but, in the past fortnight, she'd had it cropped alarmingly short – a shave, almost – and she was relishing the notoriety which the crew-cut had brought her. "Some blokes will go for this," she had crowed to the other girls. "You'll see, they'll pay twice as much."

I had already agreed to take my refs with the night-watchman at the Co-Op. He was a long way from being a perfect cook but I had known few people who could make things in one saucepan taste as good. Rabbit curry was on the menu that night. We managed to get through the supper without mentioning the murder. He played last week's broadcast of Friday Night is Music Night which he had recorded on one of the new cassette machines. He kept insisting that it didn't sound as crisp as a reel to reel tape recorder (more wow than flutter, he said) but I couldn't tell the difference and, to be honest, I didn't think he could either. By half past nine, I was dawdling up Goodladies Road again.

At five to ten, Soapy Berkeley was thrown out of the Admiral for the second time. He ripped his trousers as he fell into the gutter and grazed his forehead and he was still cursing loudly as he came stumbling along the alley at the side of Marjie's, intent on getting some free pie and peas.

"You're drunk, Soapy," I said.

"Not since '49," he slurred. "Have you once seen me drunk since then?"

"Not once," I agreed, to humour him.

The knock on his head had left him dizzy and unable to focus. "Come on, my old friend, let's sit you down for something hot and a smoke." I took him into her back yard and berthed him against the swill bins. I allowed the kitchen ladies to have their say, calling and complaining through the window, but it wasn't long before they brought us some tea.

I had already missed my ten-fifteen point. I stood at the gate and looked up the alley, towards the junction. Black Layna was there (she usually stood by the pirate taxi rank, behind the Council House) and Betty 'Slowly' Barnes (her hair in a mess, her clothes askew) but Timberdick hadn't been on the pavement since I'd got back from the curry in the Co-Op.

"She's upstairs with Wierdie Wonder," Soapy observed.

"Wonder Eversley?" I queried, glancing at the top windows.

"Do you know anyone else called Wonder?"

Miss Eversley was in her fifties and lived with her brother next to the PDSA hospital. I hadn't spoken to the pair for years but there had been a time when Seraphin was a radical light in our local Labour party and I had been one of his disciples.

"He was a bad influence on you," said Soapy. He bent his shoulders, gripped his stomach and tried to belch but it wouldn't come. "Stop looking up at the window, Ned, and listen to me. Oh God, I can feel myself going."

His eyes rolled, his neck jerked backwards and, with a groan from the depths, he went sideways. Off the step and onto the concrete path. At first, I thought this was no worse than a deserving case of Drunk and Incapable. I saw that he had cut his forehead in the fall, and he was dribbling from his mouth. I knelt down and stroked the back of my finger across his cheek.

What he wasn't doing was breathing.

I shook him. "Come on, Sope!" But he was as dead as a sack of spuds. I banged on the kitchen window. "Ambulance! Now!"

Trusting my own version of first aid, I steadied him on his side and knelt astride him, gripping his hair in one hand and pulling it back, then I stuck two fingers down his throat. He vomited at once, and sucked in air like some sort of inverted foghorn. But still the bastard wouldn't breathe.

"Come on, Sope. Give us a chance, a bit of help, eh?" I shouted: "Ambulance! This bugger's croaked on me!"

I took off my tunic, draped it over him, then rubbed him front and back like you do with dead hamsters.

Fish Marjie had rushed from the front of the shop. "Do his arms and legs, Ned," she said. "Artificial inspiration."

But Alice Harkness, charging through from the kitchen, pushed her from the back step and threw a bucket of cold water. Which soaked my head and shirt and sent me into a shiver, but did nothing for Soapy.

"What did you do that for!" shouted Marjie. "Ned's not dead. It's the one underneath."

I was ready to try something else. "How long has it been?" I called out. I put him on his back, bent his neck and got ready to pant my own breath down his throat.

"Ugh! How could you?" said fiery Mrs Harkness with the empty bucket. "He stinks."

"He's disgusting, not dirty," I said, wiping the dribble from his lips. I shouted into his face: "Blast you! Ernest Berkeley!"

"But he's filthy," she shuddered.

"He changes his underpants twice a day," I promised, "which is eight times more often than you do."

I heard no warning. The bucket bounced off the side of my head and I flew, crashing backwards into the wooden fence of the yard. Harkness was coming for me, her hands outstretched, her thumbs ready to dig into my throat.

Then Mrs P – fifty years old but still fighting fit - ran into the yard and leapt into a rugby tackle, collecting the woman around the waist so that they landed on top of the cellar traps.

Now, Seraphin Eversley was in the yard, holding a tankard of beer in one hand and his Baker Street pipe in the other. "God's teeth, what a bust up." The place was lit up as two figures on the first floor drew the net curtains aside and looked down on the battlefield. I saw Wonder Eversley look out, spot her brother and duck back into her room again.

"Get to Soapy," I croaked, trying to crawl forward. "He's not breathing."

I could see that Molly Perks was horribly hurt. She was hardly able to move, but her round face nodded at me: "Do old Soapy first."

"Where's the bloody ambulance!" I shouted.

I wanted to give the kiss of life another go, but the mad woman with the bucket wasn't finished.

"I know about you! You murderer!" she screamed.

"Look out!" shouted Perks, flat on her back.

Seraphin twisted, bringing his arm with the beer glass in a sweeping arc. The woman went sideways into him and Seraphin let out a night-hawk's screech as the glass broke beneath his fall. Already on my knees, I turned towards his scream of anguish. I saw that he'd cut something important. Bright red blood was pouring from the top of his leg in tapfuls. Then the bucket woman elbowed me and I fell backwards onto Soapy's body. I heard his ribs crack.

That made him suck through the inverted foghorn again- but this time, he opened his eyes. "I've said I'll buy the picture, Ned. Don't worry." He couldn't focus and his hearing gave him no sense of direction. "I want you to know that."

The control room dispatched Inspector Feathers to the scene. He arrived in a new and shiny area car, with the latest siren and driven by an Advanced Trained Driver. It was all very posh and expert. He left the constable to watch over the new car (after all, this was a disreputable part of town) while he positioned himself at the centre of things, and tried to compile a score.

They stretchered Mrs Perks into the first ambulance. She had fractured her hip and, for the next two days, I would have nightmares that she wouldn't walk again.

The second crew were working on Soapy. "He's cracked his ribs and he's still concussed."

I didn't want anyone to say that he'd been dead for a quarter of an hour, but dear old Marjie bawled, "Ned Machray saved his life," from the back of her ambulance. "You lot remember that!"

I didn't mind the bright young inspector knowing because he'd make sure I got no credit, but one glance at Soapy's face was enough to tell me that he'd heard and would never let me forget.

"Can you get us an escort for this one?" asked the St John's man at Seraphin's side. "He's lost a lot of blood and it might be touch and go if the Gods aren't with us." Three men were working on him.

"Very well, very well," Feathers said. "Yes, that's just the job for our new patrol vehicle."

I was propped against the wooden fence where a youth was bandaging my scalp. He'd taken advice from the St John's volunteer and didn't seem in a hurry to move me.

A fourth ambulance turned up but, after a briefing from the bucket woman, reversed to the middle of the junction and waited in reserve.

"This one's concussed and bruises," said my young man.

"Oh, good," said Inspector Feathers.

"But I'm more concerned about his irregular heartbeat. They'll keep him in overnight."

The Inspector came close. "Well done," he said. "I make it one severed artery, one cracked hip, a broken set of ribs, two concussions and one dodgy pulse. Unfortunately, no arrests but, well done, you have collected one complaint. You told an innocent bystander that she wears soiled knickers. Still, I wouldn't worry about it, Constable. You've friends in high places so they'll probably give you a medal. I hope I'll be as effective as you one day."

They put me in a wheelchair, wheeled me out of the yard, and left me in the road. Three or four people hurried forward from the crowd that had gathered. "God's sakes, what goes on?" asked Alfie Christopher, the greengrocer. "It sounded like a slaughterhouse in there."

Little Miss Dawson appeared on the pavement and announced, "It was I."

People turned and looked at her.

She said, "I, who phoned the police," and everyone went back to their business.

The crew were strapping Soapy to a bunk. I didn't realise that I was supposed to climb into the ambulance without any help. And, anyway, I was too far from either door to grasp the handles.

"Sepht-the-left said I was to tell his sister not to follow," said Alfie. "He said he doesn't want her cluttering up the hospital passageways. What do you think, Mr Machray? Should I forget to tell her and let her turn up?"

Dombey, pretending to be the local reporter, was scribbling in her notebook and trying to get close enough to ask questions.

Miss Dawson jabbed an elbow into Alfie's side. "Here. Listen to them. They're saying they're taking Soapy and leaving our policeman behind. Not blooming likely." Her other elbow struck out at Harry Whithers. "You two men, get our Ned into this ambulance."

I heard the first ambulance start up. The gleaming new wireless car moved slowly into an escort position, its beacon already flashing. Feathers trotted forward so that he could give the nearside wing a final polish with his handkerchief.

"Hold steady," said Alfie, and my wheelchair was tipped backwards as he and Harry, with Miss Dawson behind, manoeuvred it to the doors of the ambulance. They lifted, and tilted it forward so that, by reaching out, I was able to crawl on my hands and knees to safety. The attendant was still busy with Soapy. I balanced myself on a side stool – but it was no more than a padded cushion on the wheel arch, so I needed to hold on.

Then Alfie put his mouth next to my cheek. "I've had a word with your posh lady," he whispered. "The lady from 'the department', yes? I told her 'the pig shall be installed'. She didn't seem well pleased. But these people don't understand, do they? They don't see all the overs and overs like we do. The TV showing things over and over. Campbell's boat going over and over. Your tune, Mr Machray, your Kaiser Bill's Batman, it goes over and over. People don't understand that we've got to stop all these overs and overs. That's what this pig is about."

Before I got anything from this nonsense, he had been ordered away from the ambulance and the doors had been slammed and bolted. There was no room for the St John's man in the back, because I was perched on his cushion, so he rode in the cab.

"You know what they say in the East?" said Soapy as we raced down Goodladies Road.

"What's that, Sope?"

"If you save a man's life, he's your responsibility for the rest of his days."

I tried to look out of the window but could only see lights that went by too quickly. "I didn't save your life, Soapy. I bloody near killed you. Shut up and go to sleep."

"I've got to tell you, Ned, in case I go off before we get there. Tad Lausen is putting the word around that Zelda's painted a picture of you in your birthday suit. He expects you'll pay through the nose, just to keep it off the streets. But don't you worry, Ned. I've already said I'll buy it."

My head was swimming again. I felt queer. I said, "What?" and "Rubbish," and "Can't be true." Then the ambulance swerved right, I fell forward and passed out.

I came to on a trolley in a green cubicle and, straightaway, was told off for trying to stand up. When I said that I wanted to go home, they took away my clothes, wrapped me in a threadbare dressing-gown and wheeled me through a maze of corridors so that I wouldn't

96

have been able to find my way out even if I had been brave enough to try. Fish Marjie must have seen me at some stage because I heard her shouting "Tell him not to forget the Rialto tomorrow night. In time for the first house." But she was a long way off and I didn't hear her voice again.

I was left at a crossroads with nothing to look at but the join where old lino met a new patch. I could hear horrible things being done with knives and hoists in a nearby room, and an unseen door kept opening and closing, throwing a sinister yellow light across the passageway. I began to get messages that Sister Sylvie was coming to see me, but she never turned up and I didn't connect her name with Tad Lausen's shameful alibi. (Somewhere, someone was whistling Kaiser Bill's Batman; it sounded even worse in the chilly corridors of an NHS hospital.)

Then a male orderly, with shoulders as broad as Sonny Liston's, said that Mr Berkeley was desperate to see me. He took me through more corridors and down a lift. Then he transferred me from my trolley to a wheelchair and steered me around a banked spiral of red-tile flooring with a yellow concrete wall. "We call this the Karussel," he said. "After Nuremburg." I supposed he meant the race track rather than the war trials.

"He's not himself," said the heavyweight. "Going on about the state of weeds in his garden, poor sod. He wants me to tell you - and he was most urgent about this. Excited, I'd say – that the grass had to be in the chippie's yard."

The grass had to be in the yard. The rhythm of my wheels on the uneven floors seemed to repeat the list of names. Machray, Seraphin, Perks and Soapy. Harkness, Christopher, Fish and Dawson. What made Soapy think that one of us had been Chickenborough's informant?

My old friend was half way down a ward of eighteen groaning men. His was encased in plaster with one leg in the air and a drain coming out of his nose. He looked like a dumb extra in a Carry On film.

"I've got the story about Zelda Lausen and old man Corbett," he said from behind his mask.

"God, you look terrible, Soapy."

"Listen," he said.

"How do you know the grass was in the yard?"

"Don't make me talk."

But I pressed him. "What told you that?"

"What Bucket Alice said."

When he tried to say something bossy, but couldn't find the strength, I said, "I'm listening, Sope."

A nurse approached and pushed and pulled my wheelchair from one side of the bed to the other. All the time, she was carrying on a conversation with a patient in the opposite bed.

"I got it from Wonder Eversley," Soapy began.

"I never got chance to speak with Seraphin last night. A pity, we used to be quite close."

"Never mind Seph," said Soapy. "I want to tell you what Wonder said."

"How are you, Soapy?"

"The old surgeon said that I patch up good for a down-and-out. He hasn't seen a crock's tail like mine since Korea."

"Well, that's good."

"Zelda was having an affair with Chicken Broth. That's the point. Not now." His breathing was louder than his speech which meant that he made a lot of noise when he shouldn't have done, and not much when he should have. "Not round here, either. In Hertfordshire."

"Good God, Hertfordshire?" I said.

"I know." He tried to nod that people choose the strangest places to carry on with each other, but he could only twitch and suck. "That's why no one knew him on Goodladies. All those years ago, Zelda - the story goes - realised that he was Skinner's alibi but didn't want him involved so she blackmailed Corbett to cut the case short."

"Did Corbett know about Chickenborough?"

"Wonder says not."

"How's your heart, Sope?"

He rasped, and I thought the drain was going to fall out. "How the hell should I know?"

"I'm sorry. The blackmail was a dodgy portrait, wasn't it?"

"Wonder says the Lausens have done scores of them. They always get away with it. She says husbands and wives always pay up."

I sensed that he wanted to rock from side to side. He coughed and said, "You and me, Ned, we could teach them a lesson. You and me, Ned, just like the…"

Then he went quiet. I leaned forward and couldn't hear him breathing.

"That's enough now, Mr Machray." The nurse had pushed herself between us.

"Is he…?"

"Don't be silly. The doctor has given him something for his crock's tail. It's very inflamed."

"I know. The surgeon hasn't seen one like it since Korea."

"Well, it's sent him to sleep. That's what's supposed to happen." She was punching Soapy's pillows. "I'll ring for the orderly and he'll take you down to the cafeteria."

"Thank you."

"It won't be open, but you'll be out of the way and we'll know where you are."

Two of them turned up. They loaded me onto a trolley and took me behind the scenes, where only the janitors go. Working as a close knit team, we managed to get the trolley half in and half out of a bucket store on the third floor where they gave me a half pint mug of tea. I would have been content to stay there but this was only a halfway stop. The rest of the journey was so long and so rhythmical that I stopped talking and relaxed. I ended up in a rather nice sun lounge overlooking a sloping lawn. It was night, of course, so I didn't get the true benefit until morning.

I woke before five. I had forsaken the trolley and made a bed from two upright armchairs, a stool for magazines and a utility coffee table. I had been in the hospital for five hours and hadn't been examined; I began to feel that I was in some sort of trouble and the blame was heading my way. I was as warm as toast (and hadn't wanted a blanket) but I hadn't eaten since nine the previous evening.

I went in search of food. Wearing nothing but a hospital dressing gown restricted my range of hunting, but I managed to find an unattended kitchen with a huge stove that flared into life as soon as I tickled the gas tap. I mixed some eggs and flour, and dipped some rather dubious smelling black pudding into the batter before frying it all on the hot plate. For afters, I came across an aluminium bucket of cheap cornflakes which, having no milk, I served with chocolate powder and sugared water.

I stopped in the middle of a mouthful. I had already been in this dungeon of a kitchen for twenty minutes without noticing the huddled shape in a dark far corner. I knew what it was, straightaway, but stared, open mouthed, while I tried to reconcile the image with any reality. It was a figure, sitting on the floor with her knees up and her head bent forward. She was completely covered by a rigmarole of three or four brown blankets. For the while that I stared, she didn't make a noise and if I hadn't seen her hand move beneath the rugs, I would have feared that I was looking at a dead body.

Carefully, not wanting my presence to be something that she couldn't cope with, I got to my feet and stepped across the dozen yards of red flagstones. Remember, we were hiding in a redundant kitchen in the bowels of the hospital. It was months, if not years, since any work had been done here. The food which I had found had been stowed like contraband and everything felt secret. No windows, no lights, no way for other people to know that we were here.

I lifted the top blanket and revealed the haggard face of a weary woman, wearing the uniform of a nursing sister. She had the hard protruding eyes of a starving victim. Her hair was wet with sweat and her face was flushed. She was suffering from a hideous fever.

"We are done for," she pleaded. "You must make for the boats. Here," she began to undo the buttons down her front, "take my blouse and they'll let you take my place."

"No, no," I said, closing things over her breast again. "We're safe. We're in hospital."

"You must get a message to Constable Machray."

I told her that I was here, but she took no notice.

"He was on board, I know he was. I heard him talking to the Captain as soon as cracks appeared in the ships side."

Then I remembered my joke with Inspector Blake, the previous morning. He had told me how cracks in the ceiling were spreading to different floors of police headquarters and I had compared it to the sinking Titanic. Now, I had no doubt that this woman had been in the police station and had heard us talking about the creaking ceiling in his office and corridor, but here was not the place to question why she had been on the second floor of DHQ.

She tried to come out of her reverie, gripping my wrist as she said, "Find him. Tell him, Mr and Mrs Lausen are telling fibs. Mr Lausen, yes, he was in my cabin that night but only to half past ten. That's when Mrs Lausen sought him out. I have to." Tears began to trickle from her eyes, but she made no sound of crying. "I have to let him. I have to let him visit me each month. At first, he wanted money which I couldn't pay, so I said come and visit me." She bit her lip. It went white. "But then he wanted money as well. He'll want more. If I tell the truth about that night, if I tell that he was only with me until half past ten, he'll make a scandal and poor Timothy will… I don't know." She seemed to lose herself as she shook her head.

"I do," I said, taking both her damp hands in mine. "I know, and I understand everything. You're Sister Sylvie, the wife of the Deputy under Assistant."

"Temporary," she whispered.

"Only temporary?"

"He's been doing the job for three years but they've always said that the substitution is only temporary, and if they learn about the picture."

"I know." I was patting her hands. "I know, but they won't find out. Zelda Lausen has painted an unusual picture of your husband and they have been blackmailing you. Listen, I've got to get you to a doctor. You're poorly."

But she had gone back to her dream. "Zelda. Such a pretty name. There's a Zelda on board. Look, I can't go. I must stay here because my mother's looking for me." But, just as quickly, she came back to me. "We're in hospital, you say?"

"Yes. We're safe. I promise."

She wept. "She wouldn't get in the boats without me"

"Alright, Sylvia. I will go, but you must wait here. I will send a doctor to look after you. Yes, Sylvia, the ship's doctor. I know where he is and I know he'll help."

"You don't understand," she wept. "It's something a young child should never have heard. The cries of drowning people hidden by the giant waves. She could hear the lifeboat crashing against the rolling side of the ship." She made no attempt to wipe the tears from her cheeks. "Cold, and so frightened." She looked at me and wept. "We got separated, mother and child."

"Sister, no. You're not there." I wanted to insist that she had never been there (her description of the ocean matched nothing I'd read about the Titanic's night to remember), but I knew that I would hurt her if I challenged her memories. "You're here," I said, as plain as I could make it, "in the hospital with Constable Machray." Her empty eyes wouldn't let go of my face.

"I know." She bit her lip but nothing in her stare believed me.

"I've got to go and find help," I repeated. "Promise me, you'll stay here."

If I had questioned her more closely, we all might have avoided the coming chaos of the running pig, but I was too concerned about her fever to examine her story properly. I hurried into the jigsaw of hospital corridors but could see no doctor. I heard a lift arrive behind me but the doors were closed before I could raise any alarm.

It was a quarter to six. Lights were going on in the wards. I could hear trolleys rattling through the corridors and chuckling nurses chaining bicycles in sheds outside. But I couldn't see anyone.

Then: "Get dressed!"

I turned around and saw bright young Inspector Feathers marching towards me. He carried my uniform in a neat, newly pressed pile before him. It looked like something to be handed solemnly to grieving relatives.

"Get dressed," he barked for a second time.

I didn't move. We were standing at a crossroads of corridors.

"Good God, man. Not here. Get back to your day room."

"Look, one of the nursing sisters is very sick," I protested. "She's in the old kitchen in the basement and you've got to get a doctor to her."

"I've just seen her being wheeled into a lift. Covered in blankets? Thin woman with feet like tortoises?"

"That's her," I said, trying to exclude the image of a tortoise's feet on the ends of a woman.

"Well, she's in good hands and I need you on Goodladies Road. There's talk of a street demonstration. Someone's going to kidnap the mayor and dress him up like a pig."

"No one's going to kidnap anyone," I answered patiently.

We had arrived at the sun lounge. I saw Feather's discomfort with the notion of an ordinary constable enjoying such relaxed surroundings with big windows. "What have you been doing here, Machray?"

"For pity's sake, where am I supposed to be? This was where I got left. I would never have found that poor nurse if I hadn't gone for something to eat."

"If they put you here, it's because you're not supposed to be anywhere at all." He made it sound like an accusation that was impossible to deal with. "The desk has got you down as discharged or buried." He added, "I told them, not likely. I'll find the decrepit delinquent."

He was waiting for me to dress, but there were good reasons why I didn't want to remove the dressing gown in front of the bright young inspector. When I began a rambling excuse, he repeated firmly, "I need you walking up and down Goodladies Road, uncovering every ounce of intelligence about this protesting nonsense. I blame the television for putting ideas in people's heads. All this nonsense about LSE students occupying halls whenever they feel like it. It's bad for ordinary people to see. You know, Machray, there's a good case for censorship in this country. People have had enough."

I didn't see him again (until the night of my commendation). I dressed, took advantage of a passing tea trolley, then, with no clear sense of direction, I tried to find the hospital exit. Although I carried my police helmet under my arm – in an attempt to insist that I was off duty – the uniform proved too much of a draw. Hospital corridors are no place for a policeman seeking a quiet way home. I got caught up with an old man who had lost a dog lead, and a white-coat who believed that a stairwell needed guarding. Trying to look the part, I stood at ease with my hands behind my back, my feet apart. I didn't want anyone to ask questions or give me another job. Two or three members of staff nodded at me as they passed and I stood there for five minutes before a break in the traffic allowed me to drift away. Even then, I got cornered into taking a statement from a woman taxi-driver who had broken her wrist.

It was half past ten before I reached daylight.

EIGHT

Timberdick and the Mousey Usherette

Timberdick, in a dirty white smock, craned forward to smell if the chips were done. "She sounds like a zither," she said.

Fish Marjie took half a crown from her customer and gave eight pence back. She slammed the till shut and smiled at the nice looking man with ginger hair. "You're next, lovey, please," she said, then immediately and sideways, "Zither?"

"Twangy and jumpy." Timbers had turned her back to the audience as she wrapped three suppers in newspaper with jolly dexterity.

"Should you have left her alone in there? No, lovey, nowhere in town does breaded. Only battered or baked and we don't do baked here, so it's battered. You going with that or a fishcake?"

"Don't worry," said Timberdick. "She won't go upstairs and there's no chance of our Ned waking up until he's snored his way to quarter past four. Then, we'll hear him treading about and he'll be down for a slice of your Madeira cake."

In the sittingroom, the girl with mousey hair was perched on the edge of the battered armchair. Her faded blue eyes darted this way and that, and her pert nose twitched like it had whiskers. But she wasn't jumpy in a timid or nervous way; this was a lively, inquisitive mouse who looked more than a little naughty.

When Timbers walked into the room, the Mouse shot to her feet as if she had been caught being nosey. "Oooh, I do want some dandelion and burdock," she squeaked. "The wife always pretends that she hasn't got any, but Mr Chips goes out the back and finds some. It's in half bottles, dusty ones with different pictures on the screw-tops. I've got blackberries and cherries, but there's got to be a lot more to collect."

Timberdick took time to enjoy the little body bobbing about the room. 'What a charmer,' she thought, but didn't want to say anything that would stall the gabbling-on. Timbers knew that the Mouse would run out of breath before she ran out of things to say.

"I'm in trouble with Customs," she said. "I've got a policeman but he says they can't help. He says it's a Customs case that's nothing to do with them."

"Well, little Mouse, we've all got a policeman," said Timbers.

"And now, because of yours, it's all going wrong."

"And it started off so well, didn't it?" Timbers smiled and told her to sit down while she found the dandelion and burdock. The bottles were dusty because Chip-Fat kept them in the cupboard beneath the stairs. She went to the kitchen for a bottle opener and two beakers, 'though she was sure they would both prefer to drink from the bottles.

"I was happy in the Rialto," the Mouse began as they settled on the carpet. "Everyone loved me and I was sure I was good at the job. But someone said that I was showing the boys too much when I showed them to their seats, and he sacked me."

"Hitch?" queried Timbers. "Terry Hitchin sacked you? Then it must have been true."

The Mouse nodded. "But it was only a bit of fun. A bit of showing-off never hurts anyone, does it, and a girl's got to do it when she can. It's Opportunity Knocks, isn't it. Look at that sweetie in the middle of this month's Playboy. She was just a ticket girl in a club, not much different from me, and she got spotted."

Timbers wanted to agree, this month's Playmate was a sweetie.

"That's why I went on treating some of the boys with my peep-shows. Early morning was best, in different places, and usually on their way home from working nights. Though some of the day shift got up early, especially to see me before they started."

"But the Customs men thought it was all something else."

The Mouse nodded. "I woke up one morning and I'm an international gangster. They've spied on me and got it all wrong. Just because most of my boys work in the dockyard."

"Yes," said Timbers. "But it's the way men think, babe. They get an idea in their heads and fit everything else to suit."

"Your Ned overheard me talking. He's reported that I'm meeting with my blokes on a Friday morning next month and, I just know, the customs will raid our little party and people will be arrested and everyone will have to explain and all sorts of people will know and…"

"Oh, no," said Timbers. "No, I don't think it will be like that at all. No, I think we'll be able to give them quite a different surprise. Please, Mouse, leave it to me. And don't worry about Tez Hitchin; I'll make sure you get your job back"

Timberdick was right. My boots and trousers were strewn across the bedroom floor, my collar was off and I was cosy beneath Fish Marjie's paisley eiderdown. If little Miss Dawson couldn't make her stint at the school-crossing patrol, she would give Alf Christopher good notice and he would find chance to pop up and get me ready to fill in the task. Apart from that, I didn't expect to be on my feet before teatime. I have never understood that line about visions of sugarplums dancing in children's heads. I love my food but I had never dreamt of it. I can be disturbed by sounds, half heard in my sleep. Particularly, grumpy central heating pipes and creaking windows (which are usually interpreted as haunting inn signs) can provoke the weirdest fantasies. But, that afternoon, none of these familiars got in the way of my afternoon nap. I didn't hear the chattering women downstairs, and the traffic outside and the far off cranes in the dockyard went about their business with comforting, soothing rhythms. That afternoon, my sleep was filled with unreal pictures of Mrs Harkness with her bucket. "Murderer!" Who was she shouting at? My dream's camera panned every face in the chippie's yard. At first, I thought that none could be excused from the list of suspects. But then, as the action replayed and replayed, I saw that the judge's eyes were directed at one of only three of us. It was a scenario, quietly dreamt.

Then I was visited by the ghosts of Soapy Berkeley and Sylvie, the nursing sister. Soapy wanted to explain everything wrong he had done in his life and delirious Sylvia kept coming and going, recounting the last ninety minutes of her sinking ship. But even these images weren't distressing. I knew, all along, that neither Sope nor Sylvie was dead in real life.

They were good company and I slept well, with no notion of time. But, towards the end, I was conscious that my feet were cold and I was fidgeting myself into that half wakefulness that can make a chap discontented. I heard a woman coming up the stairs; she was too light on her feet to be Marjie and too steady to be Timbers. I didn't lift my head from the pillow and she had opened and closed the door before I realised that the Chief Constable's wife had joined me in the bedroom.

She looked lovely, sitting on the corner of the bed with the afternoon light coming through the window behind her.

"Your fishmonger friend doesn't know I'm here," she said. "I need only a few minutes with you, Edward, then I shall be gone and no one will be the wiser.

I propped myself on an elbow. "Fish Marjie wouldn't have minded. You could have said that you wanted to come up."

"She's too busy with Timberdick and the usherette. No, no, you stay here. There's something more important that we need to deal with."

I had worked with Lady Brenda during the war but for different departments that were so antagonistic that I often thought one or the other of us should have been working for the Germans. In those days, she was already the daughter of one Chief Constable and sister to another, and when she married a third it was with the tidiness of a woman collecting a set of picture cards in a game of rummy. Their daughter called me Uncle Ned and it was thanks to her that I was allowed to live on the third floor of a redundant training school, building model railways on the floor below and spending too much time rehearsing the Police Dance Orchestra in the basement. Matters between Lady Brenda and me were less easy. She was patient with me and friendly, but she was always cross because I kept cropping up.

"What is this about a pig?" she asked.

"I'm feeling much better, thank you." I replied, thinking this wasn't what she wanted to see me about.

"Pig," she insisted

"It's to do with planning permission," I said. "The redevelopment of Goodladies Junction. When I say it's to do with planning, I mean it's nothing to do with me."

"Well, just you make sure it really is nothing to do with you. Just lately, I've spent far too much time getting you out of scrapes. I don't want you to have anything to do with pigs. Do you hear me?

"They need your help," I said.

'They?' she wanted to ask. 'Who and what for?'

"You must know people on the planning committee. At county level, I mean. Only, they local neighbours have started a committee to stand up against the development."

She let her handbag bounce against her knees. She was looking lovely, dreamy and untouchable on a sunny spring afternoon. She moved without a sound and when she touched her hair, I wanted to move from my bit of the bed towards her bit of the bed.

"Of course. I'll speak with someone. The alderman's wife, perhaps. Don't worry." She made it sound as simple as cancelling afternoon tea. "But I don't want you sitting on any protest committees. Too much of it's going on, Edward. If we're not careful, we're going to frighten the horses in this country. Your Chief Constable wouldn't like that, and his wife wouldn't want to explain your part in it."

I muttered a thank you.[3]

"Your betting slip's on the carpet. You mustn't lose it."

"Ah, yes. Yes, it's Soapy's. Sort of shared, I suppose. Yes, we've shares in it, sort of."

She drew breath. "The murder got in the way of our talking the other night," she said.

"There's nothing else to say."

"There is, Ned. There is something important. We need to go over some history."

---

[3]   It was as easy as that. Goodladies wouldn't be threatened for another eighteen years. But the neighbourhood would have been even more alarmed if it had known the truth about the '67 proposals. Years later, an insider confided to me that a party was lobbying 'behind the curtain' for a motorway to be ploughed through our red light district. Luckily, wiser money backed an alternative route through an old cultural area of the city.

"Look, Bren. Can't all this wait? The intelligence file went pale in '51 and it was closed in 1952. We were told not to touch it again. Nothing's changed."

"No, I'm afraid it can't wait. Something has changed. Well, developed. And don't call me Bren. You know how I hate it."

"I won't be able to recall details," I said apologetically.

But she didn't need me to remember. "After the Court of Enquiry, you were taken off the active list and labelled 'not to be seen with', my husband went to America for twelve months to avoid any scandal, and I accepted a commission to photograph wildlife near Falkirk for one of the county magazines. Except, I didn't. That's to say, I did go to Falkirk but I didn't take any wildlife pictures. I was too busy having your baby."

I didn't say anything.

"A baby girl. She was your only daughter for many years, although we all know that Holly Brown isn't really Sgt Brown's, don't we? So now you have two."

"What is she like?" I asked, though I was thinking, 'What does this do to you and me, Brenda?'

"She was taken for adoption straightaway, so I cannot tell you what she's like. I don't even know the colour of her eyes or hair."

"I'm sorry," I said, "if you feel that getting you pregnant is something I should be sorry for."

She bowed her head. "You're welcome," she said, careful not to add, 'at any time'. "Identities are awfully well protected in these matters, Edward, but it does rather seem that she has found out not only that she is adopted, but that you may be her father. Curious, don't you think, that there's no suggestion she knows I'm her mother, but she has been – or may have been – told that Ned Machray's her dad. How do you feel about that?"

"How old is she?"

"You know how old. She was born in 1953."

"I hope she tracks me down," I found myself saying.

Something asked in my head, 'God, do you really want that?'

Then I was saying, "I'd like to explain things to her."

Hey, hold on here, Machray.

"That's the trouble, Edward. The young woman has run away from home. She's probably looking for you."

"What do you want me to do? I mean, if she turns up, what do you want me to say?"

"I can't tell you that."

"Oh, good Lord, Brenda, be sensible. Yes, I'm going to tell her what I think she ought to know. Probably, I'll say the first thing that comes into my head. And, yes, I'll make sure that she goes back to her family home. But what do you want me to tell her about you? You have some ideas on that subject, surely."

She stood up from the bed. She held the tears back for a few seconds, then let them go. She spent ages, like women do when they're upset, getting a hanky out of her handbag. It was too small to cope with her weeping and it smelt of a perfume that made her eyes water all the more. "I really don't know. She'll want to know, won't she? God, she has a right to know! Even though no good can come of it. Oh, tell her everything bad about me – you've plenty to chose from – and convince her that she's better off not knowing who I am. Tell her, tell her to make up a fairy-tale. Most abandoned girls want to think they're the child of Marilyn Monroe, don't they? Well, let her think it."

I sat quietly and waited for the rush of silliness to get out of her head.

"I don't think," I began, "that she'll believe," I continued slowly, to get the most out of the smart remark, "that I've ever copulated with Marilyn Monroe."

"Fool." She gave me a playful punch and tried to dry her eyes.

"And if I decide that our child – the young person who is yours and mine — deserves every help in trying to drag herself out of the mess we made for her, if I get the feeling that this is a real person who deserves all the chances, all the breaks, all that good foundation for a life that we denied her, then… what?"

"You'll tell her everything."

As she left the bedroom, St Mary's church rang four o'clock, a delivery van drew up outside, and I could hear that the pavement was full of schoolchildren sucking frozen orange juice from triangular packets. Old Mrs Harkness was commencing an argument

111

about loose change and the quality of Alfie Christopher's pears. One look at the skins was enough, she shouted. I was supposed to be on duty until six o'clock and would have had time to patrol Goodladies Road for two hours and still be ready for my date at the pictures with Marjie. Instead, I decided to phone in sick.

I pulled on my trousers, got to the bottom of the stairs and called, "Marjie!"

She came through from the back kitchen, drying her hands on a faded Coronation tea-towel. "You haven't forgotten tonight?"

"I'll be on the Rialto steps, ten minutes before the first house."

Her face beamed and she put her head on one side, which was about as cute as she could get.

"Book me off, Marje," I pleaded. "Tell them you found me on the back step, all bunged up and sweaty. Say you've sent me home to bed."

"Oh, Ned Machray, you are a scoundrel."

As I crossed Goodladies Road, I saw Timberdick hurrying along the opposite pavement. We were going in different directions so I didn't shout for her. When I looked over my shoulder, a few seconds before I left the busy street, I saw that she was being pursued by a blanch-white woman in loose clothes, called Wonder Eversley.

"Master Seraphin says that I should have no conscience about it." She was trotting along the gutter, so that cars had to move to the middle of the road. Oncoming traffic sounded their horns. Some people were waving and shaking their fists. "I should go through Mr Chickenborough's items, he says, but take no more than I am owed. Seraphin is usually so good at dilemmas but I wouldn't feel right, not with Mr Bartley's butterfly nets still there."

Miss Eversley looked like a thirty-five year old, done up to look fifty. She was limp and lean with a pair of perilous ankles and slack skin beneath her elbows. Each morning, she brushed her hair upwards and vigorously so that it sat away from her scalp for the rest of the day. She coloured it with vegetable dye (which often came off on her clothes). The colour and the brushing meant that new acquaintances usually spent the first thirty minutes wondering if

112

Miss Eversley wore a wig. Her make-up was outrageous – bright pink lipstick (with nodules), colours from the garden rubbed into the crests of her cheeks, and eyebrows drawn with real charcoal. Her lavender breath was just as obnoxious. For years, Wonder had bought her clothes at the thrift shop and she always selected the sizes so that the wearer would have room to grow into them. Her skirts reached below her knees. Her stockings were brown or black and hung loosely about her legs. She had a darting sideways look, a catch in her voice (a hiccup rather than a squeak), and if she carried cups and saucers, they rattled.

"The police have searched Mr Chickenborough's lodgings," she persisted. "They've taken the room to pieces, Mr Whithers says. But they've not checked Mr Bartley's hut. You know that's where Mr Chickenborough would have hidden any clues. Seph says we should tell Mr Machray but I want to speak with you first."

"Not now, Wonder," Timbers complained without slackening her pace. "The watchmaker's got something important for me."

"You think he's going to close?" said the pale woman. "If he's got something to sell you, he'll stay open until you get there."

A man in a straw hat was playing an accordion on the steps of the magistrates' court. His Scottie dog sat contentedly at his feet. He nodded, wide-eyed, at Timbers as he kicked lightly at the cloth cap of coins on the ground. If he was promising to catch up with her later, well, he'd have to try harder than that.

"How long has Mr Bartley been gone?" Timberdick asked.

"Three months, Timbs. He was the best tenant we ever had. We never heard a squeak from him. Paid in advance too, though that quickly ran out. And never any trouble with pets or old bits of family. But then, he walked out one morning, leaving all his stuff behind and we haven't heard a word. Three months, dear! It's not just his butterfly nets. It's all the paraphernalia that goes with them. His room's a proper little nature shop, don't you think? He always told Seraphin that his great desk was full of specimens. But three months is three months, as Master Seraphin said one breakfast time. That's why I agreed to let Mr Chickenborough have the room at an hourly rate. I do need some money coming in, after all. Which brings me back to my fourteen shillings and sixpence."

Timberdick calculated the number of hours that Chickenborough must have used the makeshift room. Obviously, she wasn't the only woman he had taken there. "He liked your place, Wondy. I said once that we should use the attic above Salter's Yard but he said he'd rather not. He liked doing it amongst Mr Bartley's clutter."

"That's why I thought you wouldn't mind going through it all. Only to see if there's any money that would cover the outstanding fees." Keeping up was making Wonder Eversley hot. She took a scarf from around her neck, made it into a bun and started to scrub the backs of her hands, like a heavy handed housewife cleaning her steps with a pumice stone. She knew that she could do nothing to slow Timbers down. "The police don't know about Mr Chickenborough and my little room. What do you think? Should I tell them? You don't think they'll ask questions about us, do you?"

"Don't care if they do," Timberdick replied.

"We have been rude, Timmie."

"Only once," said Timbers, checking over her shoulder and deciding not to cross the road. "It's how I earn my living, being rude."

"Buy me one of the pictures, Timmie. Zelda says they are seventeen pounds each, so much more than I could ever afford, but I know she'll let you buy them cheaper. The ones of your bum that she painted."

Old Groucher came out of the leather shop with a complicated bundle of straps and buckles. "You can't lead a pig like you can a donkey!" someone shouted but Groucher had the air of an old timer who knew what he was doing.

"What *is* this about a pig?" Wonder asked. "I really don't understand things like other people do." But before she could get a reply, a young girl was running alongside them, squealing excitedly.

"Our Mrs Whigg is ready for you, Timbers! Honest, she is!"

"Oh, poor Ned," panted Wonder, wiping her forehead. "Master Seraphin has often spoken to him at the Trades and Labour Club. He has a good heart, but no wits about him. My brother says Ned will never be brainy enough to be a good socialist. Oh, what a thing to say about poor Mr Ned. Do you think I should go and see him?

Not Ned, I mean. I mean Seraphin." By now, the early evening traffic was heavy. Queues were bunched around the bus stops, sometimes three or four queues at a stand. "Tomorrow afternoon, I thought. Between three and four-thirty, usually. Master Seraphin feels very strongly about his National Health Service, you see. He says it's wrong for family and work-mates to clog the place up, when the staff could be busy with other things. He says it's like stealing time from the public service. He's very peculiar about issues. He thinks very deeply." Then, "Soapy Berkeley says Ned did something in the war."

"Oh good-bloody-oh," Timbers said softly, trying but failing to mock Wonder's sympathetic tone.

Then Mrs Whigg rushed forward from the flower shop and threw a wet floor-cloth. It landed six feet from Timbers and Timbers took no notice. "Bleddy woman!" yelled the angry wife. "You're a bleddy woman. Bleddy tart!" When Timbers and Wonder failed to slow down or turn around, Whiggie stepped into the road and stood with her fat hands on her soggy hips. "That bleddy whore used to settle my Jack down with all sorts. Now she won't give him any time of day or night, not for twice the money." She shook her fist. "Bleddy old bag!"

"Leave the woman alone!" roared Groucher. Somehow he had got in front of them. He was striding towards Whig, the leather straps wrapped around his shoulders and waist and in both hands. "She's done you more good than harm!"

They stood twenty paces apart in the middle of the road and barked like dogs keeping territory. Traffic heading out of the city steered onto the pavement so that it could avoid the duel without stopping. Some pedestrians went into doorways, others spilled off the kerb and soon there was no boundary between the people and the cars.

"My brother wouldn't want me to be here," Wonder muttered to herself and withdrew into the crowd, while Timbers disappeared into the clock shop

"The Shrimp's not here, Timberdick," said the wizened faced watchmaker, without lifting his head from his work. The comfort of the warm shop was emphasised by the sounds of a hundred clocks on the wall that ticked in sympathy but would never be synchronised. One of the light strips was buzzing; it would fail within a couple of days. "Trudie and Stacey have taken her off," he said. "You could easily catch them up." Then: "Would you like a chocolate?" and he placed a Cadbury's Dairy Box on the glass counter. "I've moved the coffee creams to the bottom layer."

He rebalanced his spectacles on his nose and went back to the tiny mechanisms beneath a spotlight. His fingers were long, dry and creased like winter twigs but they worked with a gentleness that Timbers had rarely found in a man.

"The girl wants to talk with you, that's all. She doesn't want to trap you."

Timbers sat in the chair where fiancées often tried on engagement rings. "Lord, I'm not her mother."

"Are you sure about that. Usually, you swear all the time, but you said that without one dirty word."

"It's just a stupid idea in her head." Timbers said, "I don't want the little thing here. I don't want her mixing with the farts that I've had to mix with." She nearly asked, do you know how long I've had to do it?

The watchmaker kept his head down and said quietly, "Maybe, one day you'll come and visit me."

"I'd like that."

"I'm an old man, Timberdick. I have only ever made love near water. Something to do with the flow of life, perhaps. Sadly, this means that I haven't made love many times."

Childishly, innocently rather than naively, Timberdick felt herself wanting to 'make a date'. She wanted to stay here until the quarter hour when the clocks would all chime. She longed for the moment not to be spoiled by a customer walking into the shop.

"You cannot ignore this girl," he said. "She says that Ned is her father, and everyone has told her that you were his girlfriend."

"Oh, not for years later."

He gave her a quizzical look, as if to point out that she still wasn't swearing. "Maybe, she should talk to Ned."

"Bloody hell, no. He'd balls her life up, more than bloody ever."

"Ah," smiled the watch-maker. "Maybe you are telling the truth, after all."

NINE

Dead Letters

Seraphin and Wonder Eversley lived in a house with so many add-ons and bolsters that, to a comic eye, it looked like a home made up of a child's building bricks. The outside walls were a crazy patchwork of bricks, concrete and pebbledash, held together by age; dirt, moss and old smoke dust lodged in every crack. The brother and sister had lived there all their lives and saw nothing odd about the place. The shapes and colours made sense to them.

Mr Bartley's old den was in the back yard, about ten feet from the house. It had been built with bricks and blocks to waist height, with a wooden superstructure and a roof of tarred canvas. A cable ran from Miss Eversley's back door to Mr Bartley's window, but there was neither a phone nor electricity in the hut, and Timbers never learned what the wire was for. It would have been no good as a washing line.

Timbers, wearing Wonder's old slippers, padded down the little cobbled path, while Wonder stood on the back door step. The lock wobbled as Timbers turned the key and, once inside, she had to kick the foot of the door before it would close. Wonder didn't say anything. It wasn't long before she got cold and went indoors.

Mr Bartley's butterfly nets and fishing rods stood against the walls, along with a leather bag of golf clubs which were nothing to do with him. There was a lumpy mattress on a bed of upturned orange boxes, a paraffin heater and a broken chair, but the shed was dominated by an old oak bureau with so many drawers and leaves and cubby holes that any burglar would give up before he had thoroughly explored the thing.

117

She remembered the times that Chickenborough had brought her here, how he had wanted her to bend over the foot of the bed, and expose herself while sitting in the broken chair. She was sure she could remember every twist and turn he had put her through and the moments when she had made it ten times better than he thought it could be. Now, she saw that he had planned the meetings like a campaign. At first, he asked no questions and demanded nothing special. On their second meeting, he wanted know about the different people on Goodladies Road and he recounted some of the old folk tales he had picked up. Their later meetings were busy bouts of sex. He would mention a predilection, as if in passing, but study her reaction and hope that the idea might grow. Perhaps he was skilled at managing customers' accounts, but he was the customer here and Timbers' yen for marketing far outweighed his. Timbers smiled as she remembered how, when they said goodbye for the last time, he had wanted her, the next time, to drink plenty of tea beforehand.

What made Wonder so sure that clues were hidden in this place? And why had Zelda been so interested when Timbers had mentioned the shed during their painting session in the cemetery? The murder was two days old and, oh yes, the two women would have already nosed around the place, not knowing what they were looking for and nervous of touching too much.

Timbers felt under the mattress and untied the bundle of rags that made do as a pillow, but she found no money. She sat on the bed and realised that the paraffin heater was the least likely thing to be searched, because it was fired up whenever people were in the hut. She opened the back and found a roll of ten shilling notes. Only two for Wonder, she decided. She pushed the rest down the front of her mini-dress.

She had no need to search the bureau, but curiosity drove her to go over its design. She was sure that she could find secret levers and drawers. As she ran a finger along the top edge, she felt the protruding tips of an envelope, wedged in a loose seam. She picked at it until it came free. She withdrew it from the wood and plonked herself down on the bed.

The paper was stained with yellow and spoilt by oil. There was no address but it was clearly intended for Chickenborough. The writer admitted that he had got things wrong; he had sent Chickenborough on a wasted errand. Now, he confessed that further research had confirmed, beyond doubt, that the girl was too young. She wasn't the daughter of the murdered Jenkins couple, but the lost child of Ned Machray.

Timberdick folded the envelope twice and put it with the ten shilling notes. "Did you reply, Mr Chickenborough?" she asked quietly. "And since this letter had no stamps or address, where was your secret post-box?"

Life was good in Shooter's Grove. I left the bathroom door open so that I could hear jazz lps from the packet that had arrived, two days before, from London's Swing Shop. I had overdosed the scalding water with a child's bubble-bath (from a miniature pet Volkswagen). And I let the phone ring in the office on the floor below because I was supposed to be sick and wouldn't have been able to hear it from under the blankets. I've always said, you're either sick or you're not; there's no half measures.

I expected to meet Fish Marjie at ten to seven. I found a check shirt that I didn't need to button at the collar and a knitted tie that looked OK if I wore it a little loose. I polished a pair of brown shoes that I hadn't worn in months, and chose a jacket with two extra pockets inside. None of it was posh, but I felt clean.

The brown shoes were a mistake from the start. It had rained that afternoon and I hadn't worn them for three months because they leaked. The laces had snapped when I was putting them on, and the knot that I fixed them with, stopped me from doing them up tight.

I had arranged to meet Bron Corbett at the Volunteer before going on to the picture-house. By the time he walked through the narrow doors, I was already late and waiting for my second pint of warm mild beer. When I told him about Tad Lausen's racket of making people pay for rude pictures of themselves, he said, "It's blackmail, Ned. You know we always protect the victim in cases like

119

this. You should convince your nurse to come and talk to us. We'll look after her and teach this Tad Lausen a lesson. It's been coming a long time."

"I was thinking, maybe, we could use my case instead of hers."

"But you haven't got a case, Ned. You agreed that this wife could paint you. You've even taken a fee."

"Half a chipped potato?" I protested.

He took a long swallow of his beer. "Look at the state of you," he said as he licked his lips. "The defence would say it was a fair deal."

The Detective Sergeant asked for a sandwich.

"We've got nothing to put in it," said the barman. "Just bread and marge." He was sitting on a high stool, ticking off his racing selections in the Daily Mirror. "Mention it when you're ready for your next pint, and I'll put a penny on top." Corbett was a stranger in here, so the barman didn't look up when he spoke.

"Are you back on the Chickenborough case?" I asked.

"I'm not allowed near it. I made a mistake, moving the body. But I wanted time to think before people started asking questions about dad's investigation in '48."

"Are they digging into it?"

He shook his head. "The governor says why would we re-open a case just to show that we got the wrong bloke hung? And, remember, there's no evidence that Chickenborough had ever slept rough in some remote farm, nineteen years ago. Listen, my dad did a good job on that case. Skinner was always the most likely suspect, but dad wouldn't be fooled by that. He asked all the right questions of all the right people. And he trekked the countryside looking for any stories of a geezer with a game hand, sleeping out. Skinner's story didn't stand up, that's the truth."

"Young Jack Wiltshire and his chums who stopped you that night, at the end of Salter's Alley, hadn't seen the body, had they?"

"No. They'd seen Timberdick bawling and screaming, that's all."

"And you must have made quick time from the Admiral. You were seen in the back rooms just a couple of minutes before the 999 call was made."

"Have you been asking questions, Ned?"

"No," I said. "Just listening to the answers."

He looked into his beer and said quietly, "They've done wonders for that lad."

I remembered Fish Marjie making the same remark. I waited for Bron's explanation.

"Jack Wiltshire's adopted," he said.

When Timberdick saw the detective walk out of the Volunteer's side door, she saw a man who was losing his spirit. Bron Corbett was a good man who had never put a step wrong, but Timbers could read the signs. After all, it was her job to notice these things. Already, his shoulders were loose and, when he walked slowly, his footsteps were shuffling. Within a few weeks, he would put on weight and his wife would take an extra few seconds putting him straight before he left their house. He would stop listening when people spoke to him, but he'd eavesdrop on the conversations of others and take pleasure in little bits of nonsense, like counting wagtails during his lunch-break or trying to sort the number plates of passing cars into alphabetical order. Then, his eyes would begin to wander. He would find discreet ways of looking at lingerie displays in shop windows, or he would spend a few seconds longer in paper-shops so that he could take in the covers of dirty magazines. And then, much sooner that even Timbers might expect, his sorry figure would be seen dawdling along back pavements near Goodladies Junction, off duty and at the wrong times of the day.

Far off, the Guildhall chimed a quarter to seven and, from another direction, there were the shrill cries of schoolchildren as their after-school soccer match came to an end. Corbett kept away from the traffic, preferring the broken pavements of Cardrew Street and the rough footpath at the bottom of the railway embankment. Guessing that he was heading for the quiet of the cemetery, Timbers stayed a couple of hundred yards behind him, losing sight of him at every turn but sure that she wouldn't lose track.

"Knock the top off," she said when she joined him at the old bench. "Ned keeps Makesons under the groundsman's shed. He knows that I pinch them. He won't mind you having one."

121

He accepted the bottle but didn't say anything as she settled her skinny body on the seat. "Bugger. These slats always stick splinters in the backs of my legs," she said. "It's a good job I don't wear sodding knickers. This seat'd rip them no bloody end." She lifted her face so that the cold breeze could tease the tufts of her crew cut. "It's time to get your own back. They've stamped on your career, and why? Because you were decent enough to move a dead body? What did they bloody want? Maggots all over it? Now, they are going to shred your old man's reputation." She bent her neck back and took down half of the stout in one go. She paused, wanting to stop the fizz repeating on her; then she let it go. "Bloody definite, I'd say. Get your own back."

He said quietly, "They reckon the Lausens were blackmailing him."

"That's what he told me."

When he turned to look at her, she added, "Oh, we only used to talk. He didn't want anything else." She wiped the back of her hand across her wet mouth, and licked at the yeasty taste. "He said it was the usual sting. Talk of a painting in the raw." She burped again. "They've done it to bloody hundreds."

"So my dad gave in to them? He cut the Skinner enquiry short?"

"I can't say that. The murder was years old before he told me about it. He wasn't himself in the end, you know that."

Corbett nodded. He remembered the torture of separation that had ended his parents' marriage.

"What do I do?"

Timbers looked at the grass and the trees and the flowers and imagined little rabbits running between them. Never mind the threat of more rain; it was a lovely March day. She said innocently, "It's time people round here learned something shocking about Tad Lausen." As innocent as a young child spilling the beans to her kindergarten teacher.

He shrugged. "Too many people know about the blackmail already."

She began by pushing the tune through her open lips, not really a whistle. Then she let a hum creep in, and just a few words. "Himmler," she warbled, "has something pom-pom, and poor old Goebbels has pom-pom at all."

Corbett didn't pick it up at once. He looked at the neck of the open bottle and turned it between his fingers.

"Hitler, has only pom-pom-paw..." Timbers continued.

"No! No, really?"

"He only had one when I last looked," she reassured him. "Of course, no one would believe it without photographic what-not."

"Evidence."

"That's it. We'll need good pornographic evidence."

The worried detective got to his feet and started to walk around the bench. "My Annette wouldn't want me to be involved in anything shady," he said.

"Oh, and I mustn't be involved," she exclaimed with mock haughtiness. "My blokes rely on me to keep such things secret. They treat me like a doctor or a vicar. The same way I trust my hairdresser. Why, to think that Billie Timberdick would do such a thing... the whole reputation of Goodladies Road would suffer. Things would never be the same again. 'Wives and mothers must never find out.' That's a rule that Timberdick could never break."

She nodded, made a noise in agreement with herself, then continued, "I could arrange for a couple of younger girls – the less experienced ones, we'd explain, who hadn't learned to play properly – they'd roast him while a third takes the Polaroid's. A couple of days later, the pictures will drop onto Alice Harkness's doormat. She's the best gossip on Goodladies Road." She pushed her hands out to mimic the action. "Whiz-a-bloody–bang. Jig-a-jig. Lausen's spiked for good."

Corbett was still walking in circles, but more confidently now. He knocked his knuckles excitedly on the back of the wooden bench as he completed each circuit.

"Bloody poetry," Timbers said and took a final swig of stout. "And not a thing wrong with it. Think of it like doing something for your old dad. Getting your own back." Then: "There is one thing you can do for me," she said. "It's nothing to do with Tad and Zelda, and it's nothing to do with the murder. Only, I'm throwing a little party on the 24th. The Mousey Usherette will be the entertainment and I'd like the audience to be packed with off-duty coppers."

He hesitated.

"No one will get hurt," she promised. "It's just a little fun."

The detective still wasn't confident of the idea. But while he bumbled on, raising one objective after another, Timberdick was wrestling with what to do next. The murders had festered for too long; there seemed only one way that the tragedy was going to end.

She interrupted him. "I know who murdered Alex Chickenborough. The trouble is, Ned will soon work it out and he mustn't be allowed to."

"Oh, for God's sake, you two have got to stop competing."

"It's more important than that. If Ned learns the truth, he'll blame himself."

Bron Corbett sighed. "What do you want me to do, Timberdick?"

She was thinking quickly. "Find him. Take him to the police station and keep him there. Lock him up, if you have to."

He believed the urgency in her voice. He said that perhaps nothing else mattered, perhaps things had gone too far for everyone.

She watched him walk, with sloping shoulders down the stone path and through the kissing-gate. She wanted to shout, 'Don't look in too many shop windows or if you do, come and see your Timbers'. Instead, she ran forward a few steps and called him back.

"Bron! Please, one more thing. If you wanted to hide something near Goodladies Junction, where would you choose?"

"So many places," he said, knowing it was little help. "That neck of the woods is built for hiding in."

"For hiding something small, like a package or a letter."

He leant on the gate. "It would be difficult to hide it and keep it clean," he suggested. "I mean, drains and holes in walls, or under pavements but the paper would always get dirty."

Timbers let him go. She walked through the grass towards the gardener's shed, feeling the package inside her dress. Yes, of course. The dirt on the wrapper would tell where it had been hidden.

Stacey Allnight and Trude were chattering in short skirts at the corner of Rossington. Both girls were smoking. Trude kept the cigarette between her thumb and forefinger and never far from her mouth so that the smoke crawled through her hand and into her hair. 'You're too much like the mess of a wife he's left at home,' Timbers had warned her more than once, but Trudie MacAllister wasn't a girl who'd be told. As Timberdick crossed Goodladies Junction, on her way from the graveyard to Smithers' old motor garage, Stacey pulled the other girl towards the brick wall of the terraced house. She muttered a hurried aside, but the girl was having none of it. She shook herself free. "I'm not afraid of the skinny cow," she said.

"You two," called Timbers. "Have you seen the young Shrimp? I want her found and locked up in Fish Marjie's back room."

The MacAllister girl bristled, but before she could object, Timberdick had lunged at her, grabbing the collar of the girl's blouse and pushing it up to her throat. "You were quick enough, snatching her from the watch shop."

"Hey, Timbs, come on," said Stacey, stepping between them. "Trude didn't know you were being serious. Of course, we'll find the girl. Is she in trouble?"

"Would I be asking if she weren't?" Timberdick stepped back, but glared at the girl. "Both of you, go now. Find the Shrimp and take her to the fish shop. You keep her there, you stay with her until I say."

PART THREE

The Night of the Running Pig

TEN

Bond Movies

When I caught the bus at the St Mary's traffic lights, the conductor recognised me as a local policeman and waived the fare. Unusually, I accepted.[4] Rain had settled in for the evening. I stood on the platform as the bus jerked and rolled through Goodladies Junction, drawing in at each stop. Passengers got off and on, treading more wet and dirt onto the hard rubber floor. My socks soon felt damp and gritty.

"A corporation bus is the worst thing for a cold," said the conductor, leaning against the chrome banister. "Walk along my lower deck and you'll think you're in a doctor's waiting room, what with all the coughing and sneezing. I blame the animals." He stepped along the aisle, took a fare with his backside pressed against an opposite seat, then came back and asked, "What do you think? No operator's been able to stop dogs on laps and kittens in baskets. God knows what's in little boys' pockets."

Instinctively, I felt in my own pocket and touched Soapy's crumpled sweep ticket. (I had meant to post it to him. Word was, he wouldn't be out of hospital for weeks.)

"Eh, what d'you think now? Cats or dogs?"

I didn't know how to answer that, but he soon came up with an easier one: "Where are you going?"

---

4   The custom allowed officers on duty to ride for free. Neither the Corporation nor the Constabulary sanctioned the privilege; it was more to do with public servants wanting to be in the same brotherhood. A few months after this case, the practice appeared as a cartoon in the local paper. I only heard about it when schoolchildren stopped me in the street and said that the fatso looked like me.

"The Rialto," I said, "I might jump off at the stop before. I'm a bit early."

"There's an Edgar Wallace on, isn't there?" he asked.

"I don't think so. The paper says tonight's a James Bond feature."

"Ah, he'd good he is. My Renie and I went to see the latest. You won't get that at the Rialto," he laughed. Again, he went to work and came back and said, "Rialto's a regular flea pit. They still think Mary Pickford's top of the pops. I always liked Ward Bond, myself. I used to watch him every week in Wagon Train."

"Ah, well no. That's…" But he was already walking down the aisle, collecting more money and turning out tickets from his little square machine.

We passed the chip shop, where Mrs Harkness and little Miss Dawson were coping with a rowdy queue, and Weston's TV shop where the manager was closing up. I saw the Lausens saying good-bye with a kiss on Zelda's cheek. They walked off in different directions, Tad crossing the road towards Goodladies Junction while Zelda, sheltering as much as she could, followed the bus. She looked oddly old fashioned that night, with her court shoes and her three-quarter length coat with its big bushy collar. She was holding her handbag with both hands so that each step bounced it on the tops of her thighs. She was walking with a purpose, and holding her head high to defy the weather. Zelda Lausen looked dangerous tonight.

I dropped off the bus at Houghton Street and went into the coffee bar (where Fred Lighter would persevere with his Italian accent for another month before going back to his natural Essex tongue). I sat at the table by the door. The window was misty on the inside and heavy with raindrops on the outside, but I could still see the people going into the Rialto. The doors for the evening house had already been open for ten minutes. There hadn't been much of a queue and, now that the small pictures had started, only an occasional couple hurried up the mock marble steps. I saw no sign of Fish Marjie.

The Dombey girl, wet haired and close to tears, plonked down at my table. "It's not fair. I've just been told that the Echo has given me a job as a film reviewer but the first job I get is two old Bond films at the Rialto. I mean, they're not going to print my review, and if they did who would read it? It's old films."

I asked what was showing.

"Doctor No and From Russia with Love. Everyone's talking about You Only Live Twice and I get Doctor No."

"It's his worst book," I conceded, "and the film's even worse."

"I'm not even going in."

"Yes, you are," I said. "If you are any good as a journalist, you'll think of new things to say."

She didn't brighten up.

"I might see you in there," I said as she shuffled off.

When Fred shouted, "Do you wanta-notha-cuppa, Mr Ned?" I realised that I had been waiting for twenty minutes. Then I wondered if, just as I was waiting for her to turn up at the picture-house, Marjie could have been waiting somewhere else, worried that I had forgotten our date. When Fred's daughter came to collect the empty cup and wipe the table top, I made a joke of it and waved a cheerio to them both. I crossed the road to the cinema and stood by the glass showcase containing the front of house stills. I moved my soaking toes in their shoes and socks. Terry Hitchin, with old ketchup down his dress shirt, stepped into the rain and said that the main feature would be starting soon. It was obvious that I had been stood up. I went indoors, bought a single ticket and a box of Maltesers, and followed the signs to the rear stalls.

I looked around for an usherette, but none were to be seen, so I edged along to a seat in the back row. The auditorium was sparsely populated. Mostly men spending an evening on their own. The little one in front of me turned around and said, in his best picturegoer's whisper, "The little picture's almost done. It's an extra, not on the programme. Mr Hitchin's is good like that. He's a damned good manager." Then people shushed him and he went back to watching.

The black and white Edgar Wallace mystery stumbled through its denouement. As Hank Marvin's signature tune faded away, a kissing couple broke off so that the girl could cackle excitedly, "I've heard they're going to change this for Kaiser Bill's Batman!"

131

At least the adverts were bright and colourful, and we all knew the commentary. I was about to open the Maltesers when I reminded myself that a trip to the gents would be timely. Again, I looked for an usherette (I wanted to ask her to save my seat. I rather liked to sit in the same one whenever I visited the Rialto) but no attendant was in our part of the cinema. The little man nodded at me as I got to my feet. "It'll be here when you get back," he assured me in that whisper again.

A few minutes later, I met him in the lavatory lobby. He said, "Your lady friend's turned up. I've put her in the seat next to yours."

But the woman wasn't Fish Marjie. Zelda Lausen had draped her three-quarter coat over the seats in front of us, so that the luxuriant collar brushed against her nyloned knees. "Marjorie isn't coming. She thought she might do but when she thought about it, she didn't." The explanation seemed neither clumsy nor contrite because of Zelda's crisp, continental way of talking. "I said I would come and she better not. She said you'd be happy enough on your own with a box of chocolates." She nodded and smiled at the Maltesers in my lap, then she leaned forward and brought a package from the folds of her coat. "I have bought a box too. Now don't be a pest, Edward, and please watch the flick."

I wanted to enjoy the film. I tried to relish the scenery, the gunplay and the girls but I had seen it too many times before. I remembered how uneasy I had felt when it first came out in '62. Here was a fantasy about a mad doctor shooting down rockets over the Caribbean and at the same time we were facing the Cuban missile crisis in real life. I remember that the audience had left in a very quiet mood, back then.

"It's not the best book," I found myself saying as I popped the first Malteser into my mouth. Zelda's box, which she hadn't opened, looked a lot more expensive. "Do you remember when it first came out?"

She didn't answer.

"I remember how disappointed I was. And then I borrowed the latest book from the library – the latest then, I mean – and it was so bad. It was the one about a girl on a scooter and not really a spy story at all."

132

She frowned. "What are you talking about?"

"The film. It's a film of a book, you know. It's not just a film."

"Edward, I know James Bond writes books."

"Well, the fellow who wrote it did much better ones, I'm saying. He was a bit in the doldrums, I think. I was saying that I was disappointed in the film and the book that came out at the same time, and then I bought the latest paperback from a newsagent – the newsagent on Goodladies Road actually - and when I got it home, it was all short stories. This was at the same time as the one, published at the same time, wasn't very good either."

The little man was back in his seat and wanted to join in the discussion, but Zelda stopped it all. "Edward, I do not understand what you are speaking about. Please, don't pester and watch the film, yes?"

"Would you like a chocolate?" I offered. She went 'ah', took three, but still her box remained sealed.

"You made me miss my Forsyte Saga last week," she said quietly. "Such good drama about our England but, because of you, Tad was bothering me all through."

"I'm sorry."

"I shall never forgive you. Ah, I think I am in love with Soames."

"Oh, please."

"We start, Edward."

"Yes?"

"Yes, with Timberdick's story that I blackmailed the old Mr Corbett to stop his enquiries into the Skinner's alibi. Nonsense, Edward. Nonsense. I tell you, it was Wonder Eversley who made the threats. Back off, or I will see that Goodladies hears of your wife's love affair with Ginny Jenkins. Yes, yes. I am saying that Mrs Jenkins and Corbett's wife, mother of the new detective, were many times in bed together."

"Grief, Zelda. Are you sure?"

"Miss Sylvie, the nice nursey, she has told you that Tad has been doing bad things to her and her husband, and I want to tell you that it was nothing to do with me. I had no part in it. When I heard that he was blackmailing them, I went straight to their house and told him to get in the car. That was on the night of the murder. That is what the nice nursey has told you and it's true, but I had nothing to do with these things."

"Tell me more about Mrs Corbett's affair, Zeld. It's important."

"But, please. Please, the reason I have come here tonight, is to give you things in the dark." At first, she didn't move, the chocolate box stayed steady on her knees, her face gave nothing away. "You are looking at me in a funny way, Edward. Ah, I know what you want." She tidied the hem of her skirt, patted the coat folded over the seat and steadied the chocolate box on her knees. "You want to take your clothes off in front of me," she said.

"Sshh! No really, " I pleaded. Did she have to make it sound so awful?

"Yes, yes. Lausen has teased you. He has said that I will demand you naked before Christmas. But, ah-Edward. Dear, dear Edward, I can't. You'd be much too white and floppy. You'd be all over the place. The very thought in my head, it makes me poorly."

"Look, please."

She put a hand in the air. "No, Edward! An end to it. I've said no and I insist you don't pester. Now, you must look the other way."

"Do what?"

"I want to give you something I have come with, so you must look the other way or I will not be able to retrieve it from the safe place."

I turned towards the aisle. The usherette – now that I didn't want one - was standing at the best vantage point. She thought that I was summoning her, so she stepped forward and shone her torch across our seats at the moment when Zelda was trying to recover a package tucked in the inside leg of her stockings. I immediately thought of the scene of cinema seduction in that awful Bond book, and I cringed.

"Stop it, you two!"

I looked into the torch. "The Mouse!"

"Mr Machray! Please, you must stop it. I've only just got my job back."

"But how?"

"Timberdick fixed it for me. Oh, I beg you. If Mr Hitchin finds out that you've been up to no good with that lady, he'll dismiss me all over again. You must stop it." Then her mouth curled at the edges. "At your age. In the pictures. It's filthy."

"Oh, go away," snapped Zelda. "I need to show this man something important."

"I will not!" the Mouse affirmed in her loudest usherette's cry. She withdrew to the back of the theatre but, plainly, meant to keep a close eye on us.

"Here," said Zelda, pressing two small packets into my hand, "Read these at once."

I put my hand up and, when the Mousey Usherette returned, I asked for her torch. "I can't see what Mrs Lausen is showing me."

"No!"

"Stop being foolish, young woman. You're in enough trouble as it is. Now, lend me your torch." I took it out of her hand.

When I didn't open the package immediately, Zelda pushed me in the ribs. "Why do you wait?"

Dr No had reached the scene where Ursula Andress emerges from the ocean, wearing a dagger in her bikini belt. The audience was rapt and even the usherette, although she had watched the scene several times before, couldn't keep her eyes from the screen. I was in two minds: I didn't doubt that Zelda had handed over some important letters – but they would still be here after 007's introduction to Honeychile Rider, whereas if I read the letters first, I would miss the moment on the screen.

"Don't be a damn-silly dunce, man," Zelda persisted, "Read the letters."

As I unwrapped the first packet, I was conscious that the Mousey Usherette was leaning towards me, Miss Dombey was in the end seat of the next sector, so as the Mouse looked over my shoulder, her back end was pushed towards Dombey. I was sure that a ticklish look was on the Mouse's face and I couldn't get rid of the notion that Dombey had a hand up the girl's skirt.

"Edward, the letters," prompted Zelda.

135

Certainly, the Mouse was leaning forward more than she needed to, and Dombey was seated askew, half in the aisle. And I could only see one of her hands.

"Oh, please don't," the Mouse said. "Please, Mr Machray, don't shine the torch around. Keep it down on the letters."

The first was written on blue notepaper with a matching envelop. The writer was answering questions that Chickenborough had posed in a previous letter. It confirmed that Mr and Mrs Jenkins' children had been taken to Canada after their father's murder. I guessed that the letter was from someone acting as Chickenborough's controller, but there was no return address and only one letter for a signature. M.

"M," I said, and looked up at the James Bond picture. "M?"

The second package contained a dozen snapshots, taken recently on Goodladies Road. Some were clear, some were fuzzy but they all showed the young girl whom Timberdick called the Shrimp.

"Quietly, Zelda, tell me where you got these."

"Timberdick told me that she used to meet Mr Chickens-borough – used to 'snitch', she says – in the Eversley's back shed, so I spoke with Wonder and we searched it together. We found no money but we found these."

"Why have you given them to me?"

"Because we need your help, Edward. It is clear that Chickens-borough and his boss had exchanged many more letters and probably more photographs but Wonder and I cannot work out where they hide them. I told Wonder, we'll go to Ed Machray because he is our best policeman, and he'll think it out."

The Mouse was nodding. "You mean, work it out," she corrected softly.

"But Wonder said tell Timberdick, not Ned," said Zelda and the Mouse nodded at that too.

"Zelda, this is important," I said. "You must answer truthfully."

"Of course. How else would I answer?"

"At the time of the old murders."

"Yes. '48, yes?"

"Who was Mr Jenkins' girlfriend?"

"Ah, girlfriend." She started to fidget with the chocolate box. She considered opening it, picked idly at the cellophane but let it be. "Girlfriend is a very broad term, Edward. It can mean different things to different ears."

"Zelda, we both know your answer. Who was the Jenkins husband seeing more than any other?"

"Yes, you know," she said sombrely.

"Yes, it's obvious," whispered the Mouse.

Dombey, sensing the whiff of a drama, was already on her feet. "Come on, we've got to find her. She's in danger."

"Yes," repeated Zelda. "More than any other, in those days, it was Timberdick."

The four of us rushed along the back of the stalls and down the broad shallow staircase, but when we reached the street only Dombey was with me. I grabbed her sleeve as we stepped on and off the kerb.

"Get me a taxi, Dombey. We've no time to lose."

"Don't call me Dombey, Ned. Everyone does that. Call me Gwendolyn."

"Better still, flag down a police car." I looked up and down the road. "God, you can never find one when you need one." Then, irritably: "Stop going on about nothing, Dombey. I've got to get to the old playground. The wet rec."

A couple of youngsters had been studying the pictures in the glass showcase. They caught up with us as we were ready to cross the road. "Is it fruity, Mister?"

I wanted to say that it was no better than the book, but Dombey was already pushing me into the middle of the road, playing skittles with the traffic. She tried to flag down the first two cars, but only a bicycle pulled into the kerb. Then I called out that a police car was two hundred yards away. But it turned right into a side street. We were standing in puddles and my socks were getting wet again.

"This is useless!" she shouted. So she stood, full frontal, in front of a double decker bus and, ignoring the abuse from the driver, we both jumped aboard.

137

"You two needn't think you're here for a free ride," said the conductor "I know you're a policeman, Mr Mach, but I don't subscribe. I don't subscribe at all. You're off duty and you think, just because you're a couple of bobbies, you can jump on and off as you like."

When Dombey explained that she wasn't a policewoman, it added fuel to the fire.

"Ah! Hoping to trick me, were you? Well, you can't! That's two ninepences."

"But you don't know where we want to go," Dombey protested.

"Makes no difference. This close to the depot, anywhere is ninepence. Come on. Who's paying?" He rubbed his fingertips. "One shilling and sixpence."

"We want to go to the wet rec, or if not there, police headquarters," I said.

"The wet rec? We've not stopped there in years."

"The nick, then."

"Ah! Well, you can't. This is the 7A not the 7, so we don't go past the station." Quickly, he churned the ticket machine and tore off two slips of paper. "I can't refund it now that I've issued the tickets. Come on." This time, he played 'round the garden' on an open palm. "One and six!"

The bus leaned as it curved around an island, throwing Dombey and I into a seat. "I don't understand. Why the wet rec?" she asked.

"Because of the oil and yellow paint on those photographs. They had been hidden in the old air raid shelter at the wet rec. I left the cans of yellow paint there myself after the Affair of the Dead Man's Supper in 1958. That's where they got dirty."

"And you think Timbers has gone there to look for them?"

"I'm sure," I said. "Chickenborough's murderer will be waiting for her."

Dombey straightened herself in the seat. "Are you going to explain it to me?"

"Draw a family tree in your head," I said.

"No, I mean about the paint."

"Look, that doesn't matter. Think about Mrs Jenkins and her lover."

"Yes, Joe Skinner."

"Then think about Mr Jenkins and his lover."

"Timberdick, you think."

"Mr and Mrs Jenkins are murdered. There's no need to murder Skinner because he got hung. That means Timberdick is next."

"I see! Mr Chickenborough found this out, so the murderer killed him before he could talk. Oh my God, Ned, it's all my fault. When I chased old Groucher after the marbles match, I was drawing everyone away from Goodladies Junction and Salter's Yard. I was giving the killer just what he wanted. An empty street to murder in."

"No, no," I said. "Sylvia Rivers is at the bottom of this. I'm sure she was Chickenborough's informant. If that's a fact, everything slots into place."

The bus braked and we both fell forward.

"This is it," shouted the conductor. "As close as any bus gets to the wet rec, these days. You'll have to walk the rest."

ELEVEN

Mrs Harkness Speaks Out

It was ten o'clock and the rain hadn't stopped. Timberdick was sheltering in the doorway of a disreputable barbershop in Cardrew Street. No lights were on but she could hear a family of men without women persuading the youngest brother not to rob aluminium from the national freight yard. They had no qualms about the criminality, but the more canny brothers were sure that one of their barbershop customers was passing information to the police. Timbers remembered how, back in the fifties, the father had paid her well to take a young soldier upstairs while he went through the lad's wallet and grip case. But Timbers and the old man hadn't been friends for years.

The smart Rover was still parked by the kerb, forty yards from the telephone kiosk. It had been driving around Goodladies Junction for two days but no one had recognised its owner. There was no luggage on the back seat, nothing had been slipped discreetly beneath the front seats and the tax disc, although current, belonged to a different vehicle. Timberdick was waiting for the phone to summon her to the callbox.

Stacey and Trudie were larking about at the corner. They pushed and slapped each other, pretended to nearly fall over, and squealed like kids when they trod in the gutters and shallow puddles. Lights from the traffic on the main road gave their faces and bare legs a peculiar radiance in the rain. Trudie had already snitched three passing drivers – and Timbers had been watching for less than forty minutes – and it wouldn't be long before another bloke was attracted by their comic antics. The girls looked like fun.

Still, the phone didn't ring. Timbers fingered the worn envelope in her jacket pocket. She was sure that it had been lodged somewhere close to Smither's Garage – how else could it have been stained with diesel oil and yellow paint? But she wouldn't explore the place until she knew more about the car. If the owner was watching and if he had anything to do with the letter, then he had something to do with the murder.

"Stop blaming the pig!" shouted the barber's apprentice. Timbers heard the clatter of discarded beer mugs as the men went from the front room. "Pig!" repeated the young man, further away now. "Because of the pig! All the time, the pig!"

At last, the phone was ringing. The two girls looked down the street and saw Timbers trotting through the rain. A light went on in the barber's bedroom and curtains parted an inch or two. But the bulb was broken in the kiosk so there was no point in people watching longer.

"The car's not stolen," Bron Corbett reported. "But I can't go any further without a proper reason for asking."

Timberdick persisted.

But Corbett wouldn't be pressed. "Look, I don't care what rules Ned has broken for you in the past. You asked me, not him, and I can't tell you anything except it's not stolen and it's booked to a fleet in Weybridge. Yes, it's a hire car probably, or it usually runs on trade plates. Look, Timberdick, I can't ask any more questions about it, not without telling Records what I'm about."

Timberdick put the phone back on its cradle but kept her hand on it. The barbers had quietened down. Trudie MacAllister had been picked up by passing trade. Stacey Allnight had wandered off; she thought she might try things at the back of the Council House. (The taxi drivers were always good to her.)

With all the trepidation of a spy in enemy country, Timbers emerged from the phone box and trod slowly across the street. "God, girl," she muttered under her breath. "There's nobody in the bloody car."

As she stepped across the road, she felt the damp in her shoes and the chill on the backs of her legs. She was conscious that the shaved sides of her head had left her ears exposed. (She knew that the crew cut had been a ridiculous prank.) Her fingertips were red with the rain and cold; digging under stones or pulling at old drainpipes would be painful work.

The broken down garage had been empty for years, although a chipped enamel sign still promised excellent repairs and resprays. Not so long ago, the vacant accommodation had been a welcome venue for the girls who worked Goodladies Road. There was a furnished office and a sleeping room at the back which mechanics had used in the old days. Chains and hoists in the workshop meant that 'Empty Smithers' had developed into a well known torture chamber for the bullying mistresses to bring their wayward gentlemen. But leaking pipes, broken hinges and smashed windows had prompted them to find better theatres. Then the drunks and rough-sleepers had moved in, until one too many bonfires had persuaded the absent owners to change the locks and reinforce the bolts and bars.

As she stepped onto the old forecourt, the lights from the main road disappeared and anyone looking from the houses would have lost her in the shadows. At first, she dawdled with her head down and her hands curled. She could have been waiting for someone or just wasting time. She felt every stone beneath her feet, every whisper of draughts from the old eaves and the sounds of water trickling down a fractured wall. It was years since she had trod across this cracked tarmac and it wasn't difficult to drive away the old ghosts of shabby men that she had brought here. Each time, she had taken their money and a little piece of their soul and sent them away disregarded. She saw some of their faces, but no more than three, and none of them spoke to her.

Years ago, someone had daubed yellow paint around the bottom half of a drainpipe. The paint had flaked and fallen into the dirt, mixing with old grease and oil. This, where cracked brickwork had come apart, was Chickenborough's 'dead letterbox'.

Then, before she could stoop down or reach forward for the hidey hole, she heard the coarse shrieking of Dombey's sow. The sound ripped through the night air. In a back yard some fifty yards away, the animal was being coerced or tormented and she meant everyone to know that she would get her own back. The pig would have the last word.

"I have been waiting for someone to turn up."

A quietly spoken giant of a man, eighteen stone but not fat, was standing behind her. He wore a thick black overcoat and an old fashioned homburg hat. His stood like an immovable pillar, his shoulders square and solid, his arms and legs having no shape beyond the trunk of his figure.

"My brother spoke of you. He paid for your company several times in the weeks before his arrest. I believe I'm the only one he told." He was unlocking the padlock on the double doors of the workshop. "My family owns the place," he explained.

Timberdick followed him inside and waited in the middle of the workshop while he went to the office where he lit three paraffin lamps. Yellow light crept across the floor, gradually illuminating the hoists, jacks and ropes that littered the place. Timbers looked down into the engineer's pit, shielded by the crudest assembly of wooden planks. The place looked hardly disturbed since her last visit here; she wondered if the same calendar hung on the office wall.

"I am the last of Joe Skinner's family, his brother Michael," he said, placing two tubular-framed chairs on the floor and producing a half-pint bottle of whiskey from his overcoat pocket. "There is no one else to care." He intended that they should drink from china beakers left over from the old days.

Timberdick had never been able to cope with the smell of burning paraffin; it made her want to rub her eyes and stop air getting to her throat. She soon found that she was holding her breath for long periods. She didn't want to talk, and she knew that the Scotch would make her feel worse. She kept her tummy muscles tight and pressed her hands between the tops of her legs, like a child holding on for the toilet.

"Do you remember, Joe?" he asked.

She shook her head, short and quick.

"You went together four or five times, at least. Four that I know of."

Still, she didn't speak.

"It was a long time ago," he conceded. "He didn't kill the man, Jenkins. I have known that from the start but, because of the way Joe was, I've never felt the need to campaign for him or put things right."

"The way he was?" Timberdick croaked.

"He had always been treated unfairly, even as a lad. When I heard that he had been arrested for murder, there seemed to be an inevitability about it all. I was in the army when they told me. They asked me if I wanted to move to another unit, where men wouldn't know that I was the brother of a murderer. Nonsense, of course. I mean, how could you keep a thing like that secret and, anyway, I wasn't the brother of a murderer. Being in the army helped; mates were there to listen, but even your true mates can get fed up of hearing it. So I learned to talk about the peace and knowledge that the tragedy had left with me, and that meant that many men used to come to me when they were troubled. They seemed to gain a little strength from listening, as long as I didn't mention Joe. Even before I left the army, people had started to call me 'The Bishop'. Nonsense, of course. But I did consider going into the church for a while. I got as far as speaking to a vicar about it, but he took one look at my face and said that it'd be quite wrong. Me, going into the church. I've got a cast in my eye, can you see? The mark of the devil, he called it. No, I shouldn't enter the church, not with that. So I took it to be a sign and began to wonder what I was meant to do. I opened a reading room, where people could come and sit and go through our books and pamphlets, and listen to me if they wanted to. I soon had a group of volunteers and our accounts looked very healthy. In no time at all, very healthy."

With her hands still lodged in her groin, Timberdick said nothing as she studied the craggy hard-set face. She remembered snitching this solid upright man. He wore a uniform in those days and, yes, he spoke about his brother Joe. Oh, five years ago, maybe. It was the time when she had found a way of getting into the Rialto when it was closed and this man was one of the blokes she had charged for the extra comfort.

"That's how Chickenborough tracked me down; someone told him about the reading rooms. Most of what he told me you already know. He hadn't met Joe before the night of Jenkins' death. They were both drinking alone in a quiet pub on the edge of the city. As soon as they got talking, Chickenborough got worried. You see, Joe did have murder on his mind that night, but it was nothing to do with the Jenkins. He owed money to Madame Zee, he said, and he'd do anything for a man who'd get rid of her."

"Madame Zee?" Timbers reflected. "That sounds like Zelda, our gunsmith's wife. Are you sure your brother was in debt? Could he have been blackmailed?"

"Blackmailed? Joe? Well, yes, it would have been easy for anyone to pick on him. If he had done the slightest thing wrong, she could have convinced him it was the end of the world. Yes, yes. Madame Zee could have been a blackmailer. Yes, that would make sense. Whatever was at the root of the trouble, Chickenborough didn't risk leaving Joe alone that evening. He was committed to being in Scotland the following day, but he insisted that Joe should stay with him until morning. They parted in time for Chickenborough to catch the overnight express. Later, Joe said they had both slept in a barn in the countryside. But, in the end, he told me that wasn't true."

"Scotland's not the end of the world. Chickenborough must have heard about the trial. Why didn't he come forward?"

"Oh, he believed that Joe had done the murder. He assumed he had killed Jenkins during the night. He says it was only later, years later, that he considered the times more carefully and realised that he was a secure alibi. Yes, it's not very praiseworthy, is it? The truth is he didn't want to get involved." He concluded, "I thought that Chickenborough's appearance in the reading rooms might be some sort of message from Joe, asking me to put things right."

"Clear his name?"

"Or put things right in some way. I had tried to make some enquiries back in '62, but it all seemed so hopeless. I visited the city and I heard about you, my little Timberdick. You were the sort of girl who would have known what was going on with the Jenkins, so I made up my mind to speak with you. Paying for sex would have been the most straightforward way of introducing myself. There, a man of the cloth could never have done that, could he? But I did manage to get to talk with you. You thought I looked cold so you took me to the porch of the old Methodist rooms. I tried to ask you questions about Joe, but you made no sense of what I was saying. I was just a frozen old fool who didn't know where he was going." He chuckled. "You don't even remember, do you? You are a very cheap tart. Forgive me for saying."

No, thought Timberdick. It wasn't like that. The girls didn't use the Methodist porch in those days. No, it was just as she remembered it: the Rialto, after dark.

"What do we do now?" she asked.

He said deliberately, "On the night of the Salter's Yard murder, I was sitting in my car listening to the radio. The last news bulletin was extended because of the Torrey Canyon disaster, so the Home Service was a few minutes late closing down. I think that is important."

The Perks children saw the running pig as they peered through their bedroom window. The four year old scampered to the top of the stairs, shouting: "Aunty Dawson! Something extraord'nary. Truly extraord'nary!"

Little Miss D yelped, "Back to bed! The three of you!" but the excitement was too much and, the next minute, the children were in dressing gowns and slippers, running down Goodladies Road. Grabbing a pinnie for extra warmth, Miss Dawson hurried after them. But Mr Perks stopped to lace up his old boots. When he emerged from the house, Alf Christopher was standing in the middle of the pavement, smoking a pipe of St Bruno. "It's the Dombey pig," said the greengrocer. "Old Dan Groucher has been getting it ready for our protest rally. Seems like it's got the wind up. They have a great sense of smell, pigs do." The two men stood still, telling themselves they were wise enough to watch and wait.

"Sounds like it's going through the Secondary Modern," Perks commentated. "There must be twenty people after it."

Then they heard the crashing of the scrap yard gates.

"I reckon it'll run along Albemarle Street and cross Goodladies at Thorntons."

Mr Christopher agreed. "That's right and on down the street market." The two men began to walk slowly but steadily along the pavement. A young housewife ran out of a house on one side of the road and two ladies slammed doors behind them on the other. Already, a group of yelling youngsters were in the middle of the road, stopping the traffic as they tried to catch up with the hue and cry. By the time Perks and Christopher reached the Albemarle junction, there must have been fifty or more heads alongside them.

And the commotion came on them like thunder, the squeal of the solitary pig overwhelmed by the stamping and shouting of the mob behind her. Some waved sticks in the air, another a pair of boots tied together with rough string, and Jack Wiltshire had a trumpet which he stopped to blast every fifty yards. In the houses, lampshades wavered and trinkets shifted on sideboards. A bachelor looked up from his copy of The Listener, tut-tutted and went back to dissecting a poem. "Put the immersion on, Albert," said one housewife. "If we're going to have disruption, we'll have it with hot water." Others brought their dogs to settle beside their armchairs.

"Tally ho!" Perks and Christopher shouted together, a warning to the traffic.

Helena, our off-duty librarian, was making love on the bakery roof. She adjusted her glasses as she sat up and gripped the railings of the fire escape. "Good Lord, it's a throng. No, stop Seph. I mean, sixty, seventy, eighty. Really, I mean stop, Seph, and look."

Seraphin Eversley carefully re-arranged his bandaged body and said incredulously, "I think I can hear a pig."

And then, calamity. As the pig entered Market Street, she crashed into crates of stolen vegetables that Drew Derringer was unloading in the middle of the night. A volley of swedes bounced into the chasing posse like small cannonballs. Jack Wiltshire leapt up to a living room window. Archie Perks caught one but was bowled over by another. A small one landed in the lap of Whiggie's flapping dress but she didn't realise until it dropped to the floor and made her stumble. An Austin Mini, unable to believe that it was raining swedes, mounted the pavement and pranged its wing on a pillar box. Which set its horn going.

"What! What!" shouted the woman who had appeared at Jack's shoulder.

"School dinners!" he yelled and blasted his trumpet.

Derringer wanted to be away from the place. He leapt into his cab and crashed the gears into reverse. But, giving too much attention to the crowd of people at his nearside, he collided with the streetlamp at his off. The concrete post swayed and, encouraged by hysterical cheers from the crowd, crumpled. Drew's lorry slewed across the carriageway, then expired with a burst of steam and a smell of scorched rubber. Traffic could go neither up nor down Goodladies Road.

Still the chase went on. Through the pitch black alleys, down Walcott steps and twice around the circus where the buses turn. Schoolchildren, pub-goers, wives without their husbands, men with nothing better to do. Dockers and ferrymen and men from the TA. All after Miss Dombey's running pig.

At the Divisional Police Station, Inspector Feathers was passing the wireless room when he heard that his best Area Car was being dispatched to the incident. "Oh, no no no," he intervened. "Send two vans instead. We can't have pigs in our brand new patrol vehicle."

That was the moment that the radio operator caught the first mention of shotguns. "We can't allow that either, Sir. Did you hear? Two members of the public carrying shotguns. We need to take control of the situation. Farringdon's in the station. He's firearms trained. Do you want me to send him?"

"Crike, of course not. Not guns, not at all. Perhaps," he hesitated. "Perhaps dogs. Have we got dogs on call?"

"I'll keep Farringdon in the front office," said the desk sergeant, poking his nose in. "You might change your mind, Inspector."

Feathers found himself in the wrong place at the wrong time. By stepping into the wireless room he had turned this little cubby-hole under the stairs into a command post. From now on, he was in operational charge. Soon, standing behind the seated radio operator, he was taking a call from the Assistant Chief Constable.

"You have a street riot on your hands, Feathers? I've heard it from Lady Brenda, the Number One's wife."

"No, Sir. A running pig, Sir. Yes, Sir. Pig, Sir. A small group of delinquents are causing trouble by chasing the poor thing. No, Sir. Well, yes Sir. That is to say, Sir, there is talk of a shotgun, yes."

"Use Farringdon! God sake, Feathers. Get control of the situation. Farringdon's trained and up to date. You must use your resources, Feathers. This is your greatest test, man."

By now, the horde had reached the most neglected part of the city, where water crept in from the marshes and nettles and brambles grew in every patch that a man couldn't reach. Sometimes it seemed as if every broken square of concrete, every rotting timber was drawn here. The three acres of ground was a place for things that had nowhere else to go. Wrecked railway trucks, cars without wheels, beach huts with no lease. As the crowd climbed to a hillock of high ground, the old soldier at the head of the posse yelled, "She's heading for the folly sheds. Spread out! One section, cover the far side. A picket on every corner!" As the different lines of citizens deployed, he saw for the first time that many were carrying flaming faggots. It all had the whiff of frenzy.

Back in the radio room, Feathers was taking another call.

"I've found it!" bellowed the Assistant Chief. "I don't mean the pig. I mean the paper. I knew I had seen something in one of the journals, and now I have it. It's about pigs. They have a great sense of smell, Feathers. Feathers, are you taking this in? Pigs have a highly developed sense of smell. I'll wager your pig's got scent of something. Now, all you have to do is find out what usually attracts her, then you'll have the source that she's running to. Feathers, is the radio room the right place for you? Do you feel it, man? Do you feel in the right place?"

Brian Feathers knew that the new patrol car was ready to take him to the scene, but every instinct told him that leaving the police station would be the wrong path to take. Yet, he couldn't help thinking that the ACC's question was an implied criticism. He backed away from the radio room, walked up and down the passage, then slipped downstairs to the canteen where, alone, he sat in a corner and drank tea. Ten minutes later, the desk sergeant authorised the deployment of the firearms officer and telephoned a stand-by inspector. They agreed that the sergeant would remain at the radio until the inspector arrived at the scene of the crime. It was the inspector who asked if the girl called Timberdick was involved.

Billie Elizabeth 'Timberdick' Woodcock had stolen a bicycle and was cycling for all she was worth along the towpath of the military canal. When she hit a bump, she stuck out a leg. When the wheel got caught in a rut, she pulled on the handlebars like reins on a horse. Now, she knew who had murdered Alex Chickenborough and several others, but all that seemed less important than stopping more killings. When she reached the bottom lock, she threw the bike into a hedge bottom and climbed the embankment. At the top, she saw the whole theatre laid before her like some horrible climax in a horror film. The nasty barracking of the crowd, the burning beacons, the presence of children where they had no place to be, the sense that too much had gone wrong.

The mood seemed lighter as she got closer to people she recognised, but there was no hint that the night was going to turn out well.

The WRVS were on the scene, with tea-urns and first aid kits already operational. One call from their Section Organiser had brought an old baked potato wagon into service, and the Perks children had been promised first diggings, if they sat quiet and well behaved on the grass bank, with two army blankets around their shoulders. Old Groucher was explaining that the smell of nettles especially attracted pigs and it was likely that the scent of the nettles around the air raid shelter had been carried across the city by the night wind. Mr Perks was listening, but gave greater attention to the task of polishing his boots on the backs of his trouser legs, and little Aunty Dawson leant against an old oak tree, rolled a cigarette and reflected how proud the Perks must be of their kids.

As Timberdick wandered through these people, it was Alf Christopher who stopped her and asked about Ned.

"We expect to see him at times like this. Where is the old fool?"

She said quietly, "I don't know. Ask the bloody pig," and moved on.

A few minutes later, when Zelda Lausen – holding the hand of the little man from the cinema – questioned her more closely, she explained, "We know that Fish Marjie was looking after Dombey at ten minutes to midnight, and that Groucher and Tad Lausen were seen at the scrap yard when the BBC closed down. Now, if the close down had been at the normal time, it would have made sense that Groucher chased Dombey until ten minutes to midnight and five to ten minutes later, he was seen with Lausen. But the broadcast was extended so instead of being seen at a few minutes past midnight, it would have been nearer ten past or even later. So, it's unlikely that the attack on Dombey happened before ten to twelve."

"Yes," Zelda said. "Marjie must have been on the scene almost immediately."

"No," said Timbers. "If all of this is true, Groucher and Dombey must have been chasing each other for more than twenty minutes. That's just not possible. The old sod hasn't got it in him. No, he must have knocked Dombey out much bloody earlier."

Zelda worked it all through in her head. "Giving Groucher time to get to Salter's Yard, murder Chickenborough before Dombey regained consciousness. But why?"

The little man from the cinema shook his head and looked across the dark playing field to the grey shape of the old air raid shelter. "I wish Ned was here," he croaked, frog-like.

"I wish that old bugger Soapy was here," Timberdick preferred. "He'd have kept his eyes open and be able to tell us what was going bloody on."

Out of the corner of her eye, she saw Police Sergeant Mollie with her second best trombone. She was dressed in evening wear. The drummer was with her, though he didn't have his drums, and the Navy's best fiddle player. Timbers guessed that they had picked up news of the incident on their way back from a concert without Ned. She had an uncomfortable feeling that someone would suggest that Ned's Police Dance Orchestra should play a swing tune. She imagined the Goodladies lilt in her head, 'Who says it weren't to be apt. Owning the circumstances. We've got baked potatoes coming, ain't we?'

Timbers stepped back from the crowd until she was able to take cover in the long grass. Then, keeping low, she scuttled along the dirty side of the ditch that skirted the field. Alfie Christopher saw what she was up to and he was ready to shout 'Stop!' but something told him not to.

Timbers found Alice Harkness hiding twenty paces from the air raid shelter. She had her buttoned up coat on, and her strict ankle boots, and she was holding her dead husband's shotgun in her arms.

Timbers warned, as calmly as her nerves would allow, "If you fire, a police marksman will shoot you dead."

"Matters will turn out as they will," said the determined woman. "I promised my husband that I'd help put matters right if I could. I'm not saying as he'd want me to kill a man but he'd not talk me out of it, I know that."

Harkness was leaning forward in the ditch, her eyes fixed on the air raid shelter. Timberdick sat beside her, but lay back. The wet grass soon soaked through her clothes. She knew that more talk would mean greater chances of every one surviving this mess. "It all points to dopey Dombey," she said, "but could a three year old have murdered her father?"

"Oh, what nonsense. She hasn't killed anyone, but she did come back to Goodladies Road to find out the truth and, if she's found it out right, she's in there with the killer."

Timberdick frowned, shaking her head in bewilderment. "No, you've got it wrong."

"I know more about it than you, Timberdick Woodcock." Harkness chewed on her pursed lips. "I'm going to kill the bastard before that poor woman gets herself deeper in trouble."

"But, no. Ned didn't kill anyone."

"You know that, do you?"

"Oh God, I know Ned. He wouldn't... "

"Wouldn't he? Has he killed before?"

"Yes, but that was... "

"Killed a woman, has he?"

Timberdick nodded but she couldn't bring herself to answer.

"Seems to me he found a taste for it," said Harkness.

152

"But in the war," Timbers argued. "He had to and, God, it haunts him. That's why he's the way he is."

Harkness resettled the shotgun, stretching and resting her shoulder for a few seconds. "Who else was messing with the Jenkins wife in her last days?"

"Ned was? I don't know. You're saying Ned went with the Jenkins woman and killed her?" Timberdick knew that she needed to think faster than she was capable of. Oh God, she needed to say something convincing.

Harkness stated, "I know that the examining doctor told my George, before he died, that there were good reasons for thinking that Mrs Jenkins may have died in the same way as her husband."

"Before who died?" asked Timbers, fighting for time to think. "Your bloke?"

"Before the doctor died," Mrs Harkness explained. "Don't be a stupid woman, Timberdick. It was before either of them died."

"He would have spotted it at the start," Timberdick objected.

"He wasn't thinking about murder when Mrs went. Only when Mr went, and Skinner was hung, did his mind go over it again."

"Even then, he would have gone to the police if he was sure."

But Mrs Harkness wouldn't be moved. "He told my George that a doctor's casebook is full of mysteries. The '48 deaths in Rossington Street were just two more."

Timberdick stepped in the way. "I won't let you kill him," she said.

TWELVE

The Jenkins Girl

A slither of moonlight crept between the cracks where the concrete slab roof had shifted from the block walls. I knew that Gwendolyn Dombey was sitting cross-legged with a bucket of soaked rags between her knees but I was hanging so awkwardly against the rough wall that I couldn't make out expressions on her face or more than the outline of her limbs. The reek of rancid petrol moved about in the air.

"I want you to tell me that you remember," Dombey repeated.

My left arm was trapped in a chain with links as big as dinner plates. "Get me down, Domb," I pleaded. The tarred rope, as good as welded to the chain and the iron brace on the wall, was tight around my neck. My pulse was a heavy thud, making each word difficult. "I've dislocated my shoulder, Domb."

I tried to carry my weight by digging my toecaps into the brickwork, but the pain was worse when my feet gave way.

"Ah dear, darling Ned. What tangles you get yourself in."

"I caught myself. You saw it happen. I fell backwards." My body was stuck at a ten-minutes-to-four angle, my belly was against the wall and I could only see what was happening by turning my head. Which made the rope tighter, and wrenched against the shoulder. "I was trying to look for Timbers. I thought I heard her running towards us."

Dombey poked at the devil's porridge. She knew that guns were outside, that she had no chance to get away, but she still felt that she had plenty of time. "Don't talk nonsense, darling," she said without

154

anger, without hurry. "You heard the walkie-talkie, just as I did. You know that firearm officers are out there and you're worried they might shoot us."

I could hear her digging at the ground, collecting up flint stones and broken bricks. I thought, my God, she's going to stone me to death.

My God, one spark could set the petrol ablaze.

"You saw. What happened." I was hurting too much to talk in good sentences. "I caught my arm. In the chain."

"How good that it should end in a place like this. Places like this don't listen. They don't hear 'please' or 'sorry'. They know that the arguments are over and done with and whatever is left is bound to be right. Timberdick isn't coming, darling. I'm afraid you've guessed the wrong pot of paint. I don't know where she's gone to find hers but, don't worry, she'll come to no harm. The murderer isn't looking for her."

"I'm not sure I can stand this," I whined. I could find no way of relieving the pain. "Please, Domb. Get me down."

"You were so nearly right when you asked me to draw the family tree in my head. The mother, the father, both with their lovers. Oh yes, my father was a good customer for Timberdick, but they weren't the important people."

The moonlight kept shifting. I looked up at the crack in the wall and listened hard for any sound that help might be coming.

"I almost don't want to kill you, darling." That phoney word had creepy malice in it now. "I've been thinking about it all night and twice I've decided not to. Bad luck for you, I always changed my mind. You see, those people out there, pointing that gun at us, really make no difference. Even if they did shoot I'd put a lighter over this pudding before I died. You'll die, just like me."

I heard her stirring the porridge. The flopping sound as the rags slapped down in the petrol sent tremors through my muscles.

"Anyway," she said. "They're not going to kill me because the idea's still too new to them. Who will it be, Ned? Some copper with a long nose who learned to fire guns in the army, and now he's got a home with a wife and children. Those children, they think that

155

he could never kill. No, he's not going to shoot at us. The idea hasn't taken over yet; he's still sensible. These people who talk about guns and murder, they really don't know the first thing about it. Me? Well, I've grown up knowing that I would probably have to kill four people. Oh, no, no, no, I don't call it destiny. I don't believe in such nonsense. No, I say it's all about right and wrong; I call it my duty."

Then a new wave of anger came through her voice. "Who said that I shouldn't have a happy childhood? Other children did. They played in the streets and ran home from school. But poor Gwendolyn always had a past. She had her history that would never leave her."

Bitterness showed in the way she was smacking the petrol mix. "I don't know how old I was before I realised that my mother had been on the game. I have always been able to picture her going with men in the street or welcoming them at our back door or shouting at me when I peeped in her busy bedroom. S'funny how, when you get older and you understand more, you add pictures that you can't possibly remember, but you know they are true. Sweet little Gwennie had to watch her parents fighting. Fighting drunk, both of them, sometimes. And playing around. First, I saw mummy with her lovers, but didn't know what it meant, of course. Then, when I was older, people told me that daddy had his women. I mean, dad had so many that they came and went too fast to be called real lovers. Timberdick would have so many different words for them, wouldn't she? Whatever stories I heard, I knew they were true. You know, it really is strange how quickly I understood what playing around meant. I think I must have always known."

I was on the point of fainting. My head was drenched with sweat. I tried to calculate my chances. 'When the porridge explodes,' I thought, loud enough for it to be a mutter, 'she will take most of the blast. I will be pressed, face first, against the wall, farthest from the explosion. Oh God, this is nonsense.' You've been in tight spots before, Ned. Remember the rules. Keep alert. Don't try to do things you can't manage. Use every sense. Listen. Smell. Look. What can you learn by touching the wall? Oh God, it's all nonsense.

"I always understood that mummy and daddy ought to die." She almost had a sing-song in her voice now. "The idea was in my head for only a few days before mummy went into hospital and didn't come out. Every one said it was very sad because she had been so poorly. She was so poorly, Gwen dear. They didn't know that I had watched my father make up the potion. I was three. Yes, only three, but old enough to know which jar and pot the powders had come from. I remember understanding it clearly in my head. Did daddy's medicine help mummy feel better or did it kill her? Well, if I gave daddy the same medicine and it made him feel better, then I was a good girl. If it killed him, then mummy would be pleased with me for doing such a right thing. It killed him of course. But, ah, I forgot to put the pots and jars away so that when the doctor came, he knew exactly what had happened. Well, I say exactly. Not exactly. Of course not, because they didn't think that a three year old could do a murder. Ah, so it must have been the lover, mean Joe Skinner."

Carefully, she stirred the rags and petrol in the bucket. "You know, if they do shoot that gun, I think the spark would make this explode. Do you think it becomes more unstable, every time I touch it?" She didn't expect an answer. "Uncle Tucker has always said that sour petrol is the worst thing to have on a farm. Oh, Ned darling, you said I lived on my father's farm; I never said you were right. At first the family sent me to Canada. I stayed there until I was eighteen, then I ran home to England and begged Uncle Tucker to let me stay with him and Aunty."

She barked: "Nothing I did was wrong, darling, because look what happened. Joe got hung. So that was three bad people who got their just deserts. I thought, little Gwendolyn's right. God is telling her that she must put things right."

I was close to tears, close to panic, close to that moment when your soul gives in and your body takes over. Flight or fight? I could do neither.

"Do you know what it's like for a young girl to see her mother having sex with a man between two dustbins?" Dombey was saying. "It's disgusting, Ned darling. But I didn't know who it was – who you were – for years and years. Until I came back to Goodladies

157

Road and Fish Marjie told me. Just popped it out, she did. She didn't recognise me; she didn't know what she was saying. Me? I wasn't even after you, not then. I came here to keep Chickenborough quiet, that's all."

I didn't hear myself ask, "How did you know about him?" but I knew the question was in my head.

"Your Mousey Usherette. One of her fancy blokes was my Uncle Tucker's stockman and I heard him telling the tractor lad that an American with one finger was asking questions about your Mouse on Goodladies Road. It made more sense to me than it did to him." She laughed. "I was Chickenborough's informant, Ned darling. No Sister Sylvia or any of the other names you came up with. Do you see, darling, how it was all meant to be? Chickenborough came to Goodladies Road, the only man who could say Joe Skinner hadn't killed my daddy. Oh, we couldn't let that happen. All those questions being asked again. Do you think he was sent to me, so I could kill him? Groucher really did hit me hard, you know. I wasn't unconscious but when I heard him shout 'I've knocked the lassie out' I saw my chance. I ran to Salter's Yard while everyone was running through the other streets. I threw a brick at Chickenborough's head and ran back in time for Fish Marjie to nurse me."

You did more than throw a brick at him, I thought. You crashed it against his skull several times and stamped on him.

"For years, I had known that one day the man with funny fingers would come looking for me, wanting to say that Mr Skinner never killed anyone, and I would have to deal with him. I thought it would be difficult, because how could I be angry with him? But – ah, duty again – if I didn't do him in, he would spoil things before I had finished my work."

She went back to the devil's porridge, sat cross-legged again, and set the bucket in the middle. "Oh, do I really want to kill you? I've come so far and, I'm tired, darling. Really, really tired. Just one more murder to do, Gwennie. Just one more thing to put right."

Then she began to walk towards me. I was hardly conscious. Slowly, I was strangling myself. I seemed to have my eyes open for only five seconds in every ten. When she was inches from me, I saw that she was naked and warlike with her thatch of wild hair and her full breasts tinted by the moonlight.

Make sense of things, Ned. Of course, the rags in the bucket had been her own clothes. The shifts in the moonlight had been when she stood up or knelt down to undress.

"You know what I shall do, darling? I think I shall rape you, and when we are close together I shall hang all my weight on your head so that your neck bends on the chain until it cracks. I nearly did it when you fell from Fish Marjie's roof. You were choking on your torn shirt sleeve and a little voice in my head said, 'Do it now. Break his neck, so easily. Just bend his neck and swing with all your weight.' But I put the bad voice behind me. I knew it wasn't time. I knew that it was too early for you to have the right pictures in your head." She said determinedly, "It has to be right. You can't go killing people if it's not right."

"Domb, please."

She mimicked me.

"Tell me you remember, darling," she said as she braced both her arms around my shoulders. "Tell me you can picture mummy and you. Really, darling. It's important that is the last picture in your head."

With a thumb and finger nails at each cheek she pinched my face and tried to wrap her strong thighs around my body. "Don't you say sorry?" she said. "Not one whisper of remorse?"

The wall brace gave no more than an inch as the weight of our two bodies tested the old cement. She was tearing at my trousers with a stone, pointed like a stone-age axe. "Come on," she whispered from the back of her taut throat. "Whistle the tune with me. Whistle Kaiser Bill's Batman."

I was fighting for consciousness now. My eyes could see wide and everything but they couldn't hold the images. Sounds kept intruding. Sounds of Harkness shouting, 'Murderer!' Sounds of Silvie's ship sinking. But they were sounds from a far off room. 'She's going,' shouted Campbell in the Bluebird. 'She's going. I'm almost on my back!' Gibson was calling to dambuster Maudslay, 'Are you there?' 'I think so, Leader. Standing by.' Then, more distantly, 'Think so, Leader. Standing by'

The Lanc was nose down in a giddying spiral, I was stuck in the straps and rookies in the tail were shouting for mother. Fumes of devil's porridge already burned our skins.

Then I heard the bomber crash and the contraption of chain and rope dropped from the wall. Dombey's back arched as we both fell to the floor. Somehow, stronger than ever, I was on my feet at once and striding for the shelter door. That's when the pig belted in, screaming and rabid. Its ton-weight head smashed into my crotch, tossing me into the air. The shots cracked out. I landed on my back and saw, just for an instance, Dombey's pale body above me.

Blood and pig snot was all over us. My face, my feet, her breasts and belly. And it kept coming, like filthy unstoppable suds pouring from a broken drain.

THIRTEEN
The Girl and Welfare

I received my commendation two weeks later. It wasn't a popular day. There was an Inspection with All Appointments at twelve o'clock, which was wasted bullshit because most of those lads were off duty hours before the Chief Constable arrived. Worse, the cleaners weren't paid overtime when they dressed the conference room with flowers and white sheets. They replaced the portrait of the Chief in military uniform with a picture of the Queen on Horse Guards Parade. Scotch Gerta, the only cleaner who would work in the gents' toilet, said that the Queen always looked good on Horse Guards.

When I turned up, the bullet was out, my shoulder was in plaster straps and Gwendolyn Dombey was in gaol.

The Chief Constable said I wasn't being commended for saving the life of a pig (no laughs, there) or for upholding the traditions of the Force by being on duty for thirty-six consecutive hours without the benefit of supervision. (Sour faces from the inspectors and sergeants in the room.) He said that I was being congratulated for exemplary detective work. (The whole of C.I.D. cringed against the back wall.) It was nonsense, of course. Dombey had saved the sow by pushing her out of the way at the last moment and Timberdick had been the one who solved the murders. However, I had been shot by my own side so I felt that I deserved some sort of prize.

He handed me the little scroll and a large cigar and said, "Gentlemen, you may smoke." Then we all stood around and drank tea from the station's best china cups. The room was soon divided between those who balanced the cups by sticking out little fingers and those who did not.

"Lady Brenda wanted to be here," he said, keeping me in the middle of the room. "But she's in London. I think she's saving us from nuclear war this week.[5] Mack, how is the Police Dance Orchestra? Such valuable work. I'm glad I was persuaded to keep Shooter's Grove open so that you have a rehearsal room. Now, your model railway runs the length of the third floor, I'm told. Don't you think that should be a civic amenity? Always important, civic amenities. Can't you find a project for our Inspector Feathers? He badly needs management experience." He raised a hand. "Mr Feathers! My constable may have a job for you."

There was so much resentment in the room that I believed the Chief knew exactly what he was doing and he understood everything that went on in his police stations. Quietly, I withdrew to a corner near the door. That's when Lawrie from the front desk slipped an envelope into my tunic pocket. "A letter," he whispered. "I think it was smuggled out of prison by one of your tarts." He wouldn't let me go before he asked, "Drinks on you tonight? Is that right?" (Foinavon had won the Grand National at 100-1 after most of the horses had tumbled at the same fence; Soapy and I agreed to share the sweep stake winnings by putting a pot behind the bar at the Volunteer.)

"Mack, where are you off to?" called the Chief Constable and I was drawn back to the middle of the carpet where he was speaking with my Chief Superintendent.

"The Revenue Men," I explained. "I noticed that they aren't here and I thought I would try to build some bridges before the end of the evening."

[5] Well, not nuclear war. On the night of the running pig, a naval squadron had been brought to attention in response to reports of Swedish paratroopers over the city. The reports were so convincing that, when challenged, a night clerk in the Swedish embassy decided to phone home and check. Fortunately, the Swedish authorities outgunned our own top brass when it came to a sense of humour. Of course, Lady Brenda had nothing to do with shouts that it was raining swedes but her phone call to the ACC had been noted and her name was drawn into the enquiry's recommendations. The reprimand in the Director's office (at the same time as my moment of congratulation) cautioned that she was already formerly estranged from the Secret Service and that significant figures were calling for her exile.

"Quite so. Building bridges is always excellent work. Yes, yes. Get on with it. By the way, the Chief Superintendent has spoken about your record of sick leave. Need to watch that, my boy."

"Of course," I said.

"Good. We'll note this as a formal warning, shall we?"

As I drifted to the exit for a second time, Feathers tugged my sleeve and said quietly, "My office. Ten minutes."

I left the noise of the tea party behind me and I read the first part of the contraband letter as I walked slowly through the empty passageway and down the stairs.

Dombey wrote that keeping a pet pig had made her famous amongst the other women prisoners, especially the younger ones who clustered around her like a fan club. She wondered if the Mousey Usherette felt the same way with all her men friends. She'd like to know when her trial was likely to take place. Could I find out for her? No one could tell her how long a life sentence would actually mean. Had I got someone life before? She said that she would never have killed me.

"You were a mad March hare," I said plainly.

As I approached the little office at the back of the second floor, I stuffed the letter back in my pocket. For later. The two Revenue Men were examining a large sketch map, spread across a desk. It was populated with matchboxes, pen tops, counters and sugar cubes. The officers worked with a buzz and sparkle but had the drawn faces of men who hadn't been off duty for days.

The boss glanced at me but said nothing and went on working, putting the finishing touches to their tactical plan.

"You still believe in the case?" I said, leaning against the doorframe.

They didn't invite me in.

"Even though your informant has killed your agent?"

The boss stepped backwards to the window and propped his backside on the ledge. He went into his jacket pocket for cigarettes. "Essentially, the murder was a private matter, nothing to do with our investigation," he said. "Dombey always gave us good information, and we have separate intelligence that the usherette is going ahead with the 24th."

"Very likely." They were already half in the corridor.

The Shrimp and I sat in two chairs on the same side of the desk. For an age, we didn't speak as we searched each other's face for clues. She had Brenda's eyes and her habit of crossing her ankles. It was hard not to think that, with a little more luck, our three lives could have been very different.